BT

D1395407

WAT

ROTHERHAM LIBRARY & INFORMATION SERVICE

R7G2

| Kollinson 1/20 | | |
|---|---|---|
| WATH 2/20 | | |
| JUL 2022 THU 4123 | | |
| | | |

This book must be returned by the date specified at the time of issue as
the DATE DUE FOR RETURN.
The loan may be extended (personally, by post, telephone or online) for
a further period if the book is not required by another reader, by quoting
the above number / author / title.

## Enquiries: 01709 336774

## www.rotherham.gov.uk/libraries

*USA TODAY* bestselling author **Jules Bennett** has published over sixty books and never tires of writing happy endings. Writing strong heroines and alpha heroes is Jules's favourite way to spend her workdays. Jules hosts weekly contests on her Facebook fan page and loves chatting with readers on Twitter, Facebook and via email through her website. Stay up-to-date by signing up for her newsletter at julesbennett.com.

# Married
# in Name Only

# JULES BENNETT

MILLS & BOON

First published in Great Britain 2019
by Mills & Boon, an imprint of HarperCollins*Publishers*
1 London Bridge Street, London, SE1 9GF

Large Print edition 2019

© 2019 Harlequin Books S.A.

Special thanks and acknowledgement are given
to Jules Bennett for her contribution to the
Texas Cattleman's Club: Houston miniseries.

ISBN: 978-0-263-08368-2

MIX
Paper from
responsible sources
FSC
www.fsc.org FSC™ C007454

This book is produced from independently certified
FSC™ paper to ensure responsible forest management. For
more information visit www.harpercollins.co.uk/green.

Printed and bound in Great Britain
by CPI Group (UK) Ltd, Croydon, CR0 4YY

Legacy means passing down a gift and there's no greater gift than love. This is for you, Lori. Your love and light will shine on forever.

# One

"I didn't know who else to turn to."

That statement alone added to the already sickening feeling in the pit of Paisley Morgan's stomach. As if life hadn't knocked her down over and over, now she stood on the other side of Lucas Ford's desk as he continued to glare at her like she had nerve walking in here.

Well, she did have nerve. After dumping him years ago and never speaking to him since. But that was all in the past. Wasn't it?

He leaned back in his leather desk chair

and remained silent, and she couldn't help but second-guess just how much her bold move twelve years ago had affected him.

Had he not moved on? Found someone else to drive insanely wild with desire just from one piercing blue stare? Had he ever thought of her? Because there hadn't been a day she hadn't questioned her decision to let him go.

Paisley had bigger issues to worry about than their past and what Lucas may or may not be feeling seeing her show up unannounced. Like the fact that her biological father could be Sterling Perry—the man loathed by nearly the entire city of Houston for his scheming, stealing and money laundering. Not to mention he was arrested for conspiracy to commit fraud.

"What makes you think Sterling is your father, and why should I help you?"

Paisley gripped her clutch in one hand and the letter from her late mother in the other. "I have reason to believe he's my dad and I need you to investigate to see what you can find out."

Lucas stared at her another minute, giving her a visual lick as he came to his feet. He was still just as ruggedly sexy as she remembered, but those shoulders had gotten broader, the creases at the corners of his eyes deeper and the strong jaw firmer.

Lucas Ford could always make her breath catch as a young woman and it was no different now, even though years had passed since she'd seen him. Her body responded just the same. There were some memories that were too alive to be pushed into the past. Those vivid moments were always part of her everyday life, no matter how she'd tried to move on.

"What's this reason you have?" he asked.

Paisley swallowed and glanced down to the letter in her hand. She didn't bother unfolding the paper as she tossed it down onto his desk. She bit the inside of her cheek to keep her emotions in check. Now was not the time to fall apart. Remaining strong in front of Lucas was imperative, especially considering he hadn't seen her in over a decade. Vulnerability and tears wouldn't get her what she wanted; what she needed.

And Lucas was her stepping-stone to finding out the real truth since the obvious choice of her birth certificate had been left blank on the father line.

If there had been any other way than to contact Lucas…

He reached for the letter, opened it up and shoved one hand in his pocket as he read. She knew every word written in her mother's flawless, delicate writing. It was the content that had Paisley so unsettled and questioning everything she'd ever known and what kind of future she'd ultimately have.

Lucas's eyes darted back to her. "You believe this? Your mother wasn't the most—"

"I'm well aware of my mother's faults," she defended. "That's not why I'm here."

Lucas muttered a curse beneath his breath. "I didn't mean that. Despite what went down between us, I was sorry to hear about your mother."

Paisley nodded her acceptance of his apology as another wave of emotions threatened to clog her throat. She'd mentally pushed through the difficult past few months. The flood that had torn through Houston had ultimately claimed her mother's life and left devastation and destruction in its wake. It had also left an unidentified body on the construction site of one of Sterling Perry's properties—the elite Texas Cattleman's Club. Even after all the time had passed, there was still a mystery surrounding the identity of the deceased. There was no ID on the person and no distinguished markings. The entire ordeal was a mess.

An even bigger mess since the person they thought had died, Vincent Hamm, had actually texted his boss and stated he quit and was taking off for the Virgin Islands. So, clearly a man soaking up the rays wasn't the unidentifiable body found on Sterling's construction site.

Sterling already had issues going on with the whole scheme he had concocted, which had left a good portion of the region's banking system in an uproar and many families had lost everything they had… Paisley's mother included. When she'd passed, Paisley had had to use her own savings to pay for her mother's burial since there had been no life insurance.

As if dealing with the financial hit of Sterling Perry's debacle wasn't enough, Paisley feared for the future of her bridal shop now that she had no cushion to fall back on. But Paisley truly believed she could salvage her future, her finances. If the all-powerful billionaire was indeed her father, maybe she had a chance.

"I need to know if Sterling is my dad," she went on. "I know Mom wasn't the most dependable or honest, but I also don't know why she'd lie about something like this or why she'd write a letter and never actually give it to me. I found it tucked into a book she'd been reading."

Lucas glanced back down to the paper in his hands. "Sterling doesn't deserve to know the truth if you're his daughter."

"Maybe he doesn't know anything," she replied.

Paisley took in a deep breath and went for the whole truth. "Listen, I know I'm the last person you wanted to see come into your office."

"Actually, Sterling would be the last person, but since he's incarcerated, that's a nonissue."

"As I was saying," she continued, hating how vulnerable she felt standing before the only man she'd ever loved. "I'm not your favorite person. I get that. If you need to lash out and deal with the past first, fine, but you're the best in this business and I need your help."

A corner of his mouth kicked up. "Been keeping up with me, Tart?"

A shiver slid all through her at the nickname that stemmed from her favorite candy. He'd been the only one to call her that, but she'd never forgotten. Clearly, neither had he. That instant reminder from the past of the bond they shared gave her a sliver of hope that maybe he wouldn't just throw her out of here without hearing her out or at least giving her the chance to defend herself.

He remained silent as he just stood there with a look she couldn't quite describe. Part of her recognized the desire, but there was a layer of something else and she couldn't tell if it was disdain or frustration.

The way Lucas used to look at her would have her clothes falling off in record time. They'd never argued, they'd had their future all mapped out...until one day she'd realized she had to let him go.

"Are you going to help me or not?" she demanded because getting caught up in nostalgia was not going to help her sanity or her business.

"My assistant can take down all the information and the deposit for my services." Lucas tossed the letter back onto his desk. "I'll be in touch."

Anger bubbled within her. He was not going to dismiss her that easily. True, they'd ended on abrupt terms, but that didn't just erase all they'd shared to that point. She wouldn't let him just brush her aside when this was all she had left.

"First of all, I'm not dealing with your assistant, I'm dealing with you." He was about to see just how serious she was about getting his help. "Second, I don't exactly have all of the funds right now. But I promise you will get every dollar you are owed. I'm not leaving until you agree to take this case."

Lucas took in a deep breath and circled his desk. With slow, methodical moves, he came to stand directly in front of her, bringing with him a waft of aftershave that smelled expensive and downright sexy.

Expensive and sexy? That summed up Lucas Ford in two simple words. He'd always been in a totally different league, but she'd been naive enough to believe the difference wouldn't matter.

She'd been so utterly wrong and they'd both been crushed in the end.

"You need me." His bold statement was as honest and real as anything they'd ever said. "You're stuck without my help. Is that what you're saying?"

Paisley gritted her teeth and nodded. He had her in a difficult position and he damn well knew it, but she'd meant it when she said she wasn't leaving without his help. She had nothing left to lose, but she had everything to gain.

A smile spread across his tanned face and made those bright blue eyes shine with amusement and something akin to deviousness. "There might be a fee you can afford."

Lucas didn't know what game he was playing, but once he'd started talking, he couldn't stop himself. Paisley waltzed in here looking too damn sweet and innocent than should be allowed—and he knew she was neither. She couldn't be, not with the way she'd pulled a Dear John breakup with him twelve years ago. That had obliterated any "sweetness," and he'd stolen her innocence one stormy night in the garden shed on his father's estate.

They'd been each other's firsts so of course she'd stuck with him. He refused to admit it was because he was foolish enough to actually think they'd marry and live happily ever after.

Now she came to him with another type of letter, this one dropping a veiled hint that the devil himself was her biological father.

Oh, she didn't come out and name Sterling, but the clues she dropped with words like "billionaire" and "well-known Houston businessman" and the real red flag of "a man nobody wants to mess with."

Sterling Perry had ruined so many lives over the years and the trickling effect would last for some time to come. In fact, Sterling was the whole reason Lucas had entered into private investigator work to begin with. Once Sterling had ruined Lucas's father, wiping out the businessman's reputation when he spread lies about stolen money and Sterling claimed to have proof to back up his claims. All of it turned out to be bogus, but the damage had been done. It had ruined Lucas's father.

Lucas had vowed to work to seek justice for those who couldn't obtain it themselves.

Most recently, Sterling's crooked investments had bankers scrambling to secure their reputations and businesses. So many small businesses were affected, like Paisley's wedding shop.

But now he'd been arrested for conspiracy to commit fraud and Lucas hoped like hell the man never saw the light of day again…though something more damning would have to be found for Sterling to be put away for the amount of time he deserved.

Lucas never liked Sterling, never even wanted to mention the man's name, and now Paisley was asking him to research the guy? Was there a ring of truth to this cryptic letter?

As much as Paisley had hurt him, Lucas still couldn't imagine a monster like Sterling having a child like Paisley. The last thing he wanted to do was get wrapped up in either of their lives...and if those two lives were entangled? Damn it. He turned cases down on the daily simply because he didn't want them for one reason or another. He could quit working now and never have to worry about making a living again. Money had never been the issue and that wasn't the reason he hesitated now.

Something pulled at him. No, not something. Paisley. Even after all these years, she had some damn hold over his conscience. He knew she worked hard for her business and she struggled now, both emotionally and financially.

Plus, he knew that emptiness at the loss of a parent. How could he just ignore her when she needed someone and clearly, he was it?

But he wasn't a fool, and he was going into this with more experience than he'd done before and his generosity would most certainly come at a price.

"Listen," she started before he could get to his offer. "I know I hurt you years ago—"

"You left a damn note." A note he'd held on to for too long until he'd finally tossed it into his fireplace and watched it burn while he'd downed copious amounts of his favorite bourbon. "After all we'd shared, I deserved better. Or maybe the serious relationship was only one-sided."

"You know that's not the case," she defended with a layer of hurt in her tone. "I had to let you go, Lucas. Your father…"

Intrigued, and maybe a little pissed at the

fact she was even here, Lucas crossed his arms over his chest. "My father, what?"

Paisley licked her lips and tucked her hair behind her ears. A slight nervous habit she'd clearly never outgrown. An instant later, she squared her shoulders and tipped her chin.

"Your father told me I was holding you back," she stated. "You were all set to head off to Harvard with a full scholarship and, well, he was right. I would've held you back. You would have put all your goals on hold to stay with me."

Gritting his teeth, Lucas thought back to the night he'd found her letter on the seat of his truck. Upon reading it the first time he'd thought it was a joke, but then he'd read it a second and third time, knowing full well his Paisley had gotten scared and hadn't trusted what they had…she hadn't trusted him.

Ultimately, that had been what hurt the most. She hadn't had enough faith in him and the fact he would've conquered anything to be with her. Forever.

But he hadn't known the bit about his father until just now. That was a new pain. The betrayal from his own father who witnessed how distraught Lucas had been and kept urging him to move on with his life and put adolescent relationships in the past.

Pushing aside the raw memories, Lucas dropped his arms and shrugged. "That's a nice story. Maybe it's true, maybe it's not. Doesn't matter at this point."

Paisley opened her mouth as pain flashed in her hazel eyes. Then she merely nodded as if she couldn't even come up with a plausible defense, which just proved his point that she didn't have one. Seeing her again did bring back a rush of memories, but even more maddening was the fact that her standing before him had his body stirring.

Damn it. He could block out the hurt, he could even block out how foolish he'd been to think they were a forever thing, but he couldn't block out the way she'd felt lying against him or how her warm breath washed over his torso as she eased down his body.

Lucas muttered a curse and circled back around to take a seat at his desk. If he didn't get these lustful thoughts under control, this impromptu meeting would turn embarrassing real fast. He prided himself on being the best, taking on elite clients, and one proverbial blast from his past threatened to turn him back into a horny teen.

"Coming here was a mistake," she murmured as she took a step forward and reached for the letter on his desk.

Lucas snaked his hand out to cover hers, waiting until her gaze met his. The instant she looked at him, Lucas knew he had her. She was in a bind and he could help...with a price. He didn't want to be a dick about this, but he also had his own wants and needs. No reason they couldn't help each other, right?

Besides, he'd given up on fairy-tale thinking long ago. He knew *love* was just a four-letter word people tossed around to benefit their own needs.

"The only mistake would be you walking out again, Tart."

Her lips thinned. "If we're done with the past, then stop calling me that."

She was still so damn sexy when her cheeks tinged pink when she got angry. Every part of him wanted to give her hand a yank until she stumbled down onto his desk where he could give her a proper re-union.

But business came first. She'd taught him that valuable lesson.

"I'll help you," he told her, keeping his hand on hers. He slowly rose to his feet and leaned across the desk. "I'll discreetly dig into this story about Sterling being your father and I'll save your bridal shop because I know you're on the brink of financial ruin."

Paisley's lids lowered, out of shame or frustration he didn't know. "And you want something in return. What is it?" she asked, focusing back on him.

Lucas released her now and tucked that wayward strand of honey-blond hair behind her ear. "Marry me."

# Two

Oh, he was the most infuriating, arrogant man she'd ever met. Of all the things he could've asked for...

Was he mocking her and the life they'd had all planned out?

Or did he honestly believe marrying him would solve all of her problems? As if Lucas Ford had some magic wand that came with a marriage certificate and he'd wave it around like her sexy fairy godfather and she'd see stars and hearts.

Okay, that all sounded fabulous, but even

he wasn't that powerful. And if he could manage all that, there was no way in hell she'd marry him. Her life was a mess and she wasn't in the mood to play games.

That was why yesterday she had simply snatched the letter from his desk and marched out of his fancy office without a word. She'd told herself she'd figure this all out on her own...somehow.

First, her bridal boutique, Lilac Loft. Paisley slid two ball gown wedding dresses down the rack to make room for the new beaded A-line that had been a special order. Each wedding was special and each bride was treated like she was the only customer. Paisley prided herself on giving each wedding the time and attention it needed. She'd had one part-time employee, but Paisley had to let her go when the whole financial debacle happened, thanks to Sterling.

Talk about feeling terrible. Paisley had hated letting Margaret go. The young girl had been so sweet, but the extra expense was just pushing Paisley to a position she wasn't comfortable with.

Paisley slid her hand down the clear bag that protected the beaded gown and couldn't help but let her daydreams get the best of her—an occupational hazard.

One day she'd have her own fabulous gown from her own store. She'd walk down the aisle lined with her favorite flowers— lilac—to the man of her dreams waiting at the end. A man that was not blackmailing her into marriage simply because they shared a past.

What was his angle, anyway? Did he just want to prove that he could get her? Did he just want her in his bed?

Paisley turned and pulled another plastic-wrapped, embellished gown from the shipment box. Each dress that passed through her store had the ability to make any woman feel like royalty, or a freakin' warrior if that's what she chose. Wedding gowns were the pinnacle of each ceremony. And while the focus should be on the happy couple, everyone knew all eyes were on the bride and what she wore. That second she stepped to the beginning of the aisle was like her own little red carpet moment.

Paisley had dealt with brides who wanted all the bling and poof, while other brides preferred short and simple. Some wanted a veil while others preferred a simple flower or even a sparkling headband. Paisley loved her job and that each customer brought unique opinions and ideas for their special day.

Unable to resist, Paisley hung the second gown up and pulled the zipper down. She parted the plastic and slid her fingertip over the intricate beadwork. Each time she mentally planned her wedding, she volleyed back and forth between wanting an intimate wedding with a little simple, body-hugging strapless dress or a lavish cathedral wedding in an elaborate gown with a train that trailed the aisle behind her, à la Princess Diana.

Regardless of the dress and the venue,

the man and the marriage itself were all that mattered. One day she would marry, she'd have kids and live happily ever after. She didn't think that was a fantasy at all. She made her living off believing such realities and truly felt with her whole heart that there was someone out there for everyone.

Her someone wasn't Lucas Ford. She'd once thought he was, but if that were the case, they would've ended up together before now. She didn't think fate threw her the curve of taking her mother away only to give her back the one man she truly loved.

"That's a beautiful dress."

Paisley startled and spun around, her hand to her heart. The devil himself stood before her, only there were no horns and a pitchfork. Only a black Stetson and a shiny belt buckle for this one.

"I'm not open yet," she informed Lucas.

With that black suit and black shirt, he looked absolutely perfect amid these crisp white gowns. Like the mysterious cowboy coming to sweep away his bride. If only her life were that simple and utterly romantic. Her heart fluttered at the idea.

"Door was unlocked," he replied as he leaned a shoulder against the back door leading to the storage room.

Paisley tucked the dress, and her fantasy, away and turned her full attention to her unwanted guest.

"My sign says Closed," she retorted. "But I assume you don't follow rules. So, what do you want?"

"You left my office without an answer to my proposal."

Paisley snorted and resisted the urge to roll her eyes—barely. "Any other man would have taken my silence and dramatic exit as answer enough."

"Other men don't know you like I do, Tart."

"Would you stop with that?" she demanded.

"Why?" he asked, pushing off the door

and stalking toward her. "You don't like remembering us?"

"There is no us." No matter how much she'd wanted them to last. Back then her dreams had included Lucas. Now she had new goals and none of them involved an old boyfriend.

"Listen. If you'd get your pride out of the equation, you'd see that marrying me is the smartest move for you."

He took another step toward her until he stood way, way too close. That expensive, masculine cologne wafted around her, pulling her tighter into his web of charm and seduction.

Hell, at this point she didn't need all of those past memories tugging her into submission. The man Lucas had grown into was doing a fine job of that on his own.

"You'll owe me nothing for finding the truth about your father," he started, those bright blue eyes holding her in place. "I'll make sure your business doesn't fall victim to Sterling, as many others have, and you'll never have to worry about money again."

"And I only have to sell my soul to obtain all of that?" she asked.

Lucas's eyes raked over her, then landed on her mouth. "It's not your soul I'm after."

Despite Paisley's best attempt at trying to ignore his suggestive remark, a shiver crept through her. Her entire body tingled and her common sense and her hormones were waging their own battle and she knew—she just knew—which would come out on top.

"We're not the same people we once were," she reminded him. "We're not even close."

"We could be closer."

He smirked and reached for her, but she skirted around him.

"Would you stop with the charm and one-liners that you think will get me to drop my panties?"

"You wear panties? I recall a time you didn't."

Paisley gritted her teeth and reminded herself violence was not the answer. Regaining control of this conversation was the only way to show him she was not so vulnerable that she'd marry him. She didn't need someone to ride to her rescue, damn it. She just needed someone to find out the truth about her father and, unfortunately, Lucas was the best in the field.

Paisley headed toward the front of her store. Standing amid stunning wedding gowns while staring down a tempting proposal was not helping her sanity. And she was tempted…but that was just the memories reminding her how perfect they'd been together at one time. No matter what happened between them, their chemistry could never be denied or forgotten.

She'd tried to forget. Life would have been so much easier if she could've erased the feel of his touch, the comfort of falling asleep in his arms.

"I'm not marrying you," she stated, hop-

ing one of these times he'd believe her...
and she'd convince herself not to fall for
his charm. "If Sterling is my father, I won't
need your money. Sterling will want to
take care of what's his and I deserve for
him to give back after what he did to my
mother. I just need to stay on my feet now
that everything's been pulled away."

Paisley moved to the entrance and ar-
ranged the blush-pink throw pillows on
the white sofa. They were perfect, but she
needed to do something that didn't involve
looking or touching Lucas.

"You'd rather take that bastard's money
than let me help?"

If she didn't know better, she'd say he
sounded almost hurt. Paisley steeled herself against any emotions. That was not
what this was about and they'd gotten too
far off track.

"All I need from you is to find the truth,"
she reiterated, spinning back around after

beating her pillows. "Do you want to take the case or not?"

Lucas rocked back on his heels and shoved his hands in his pockets as if he hadn't a care in the world. Must be nice to not worry about the possibility of losing your business or potentially finding out your father was a murderer. Not to mention trying to mourn the loss of your mother. There was only so much heartache a person could take without breaking, and Paisley refused to break in front of Lucas.

"Do you really think Sterling will recognize you as one of his own and just welcome you into the fold?"

Well…yeah. She did, but what if he didn't? What if he didn't care? He already had plenty of children and it wasn't like he needed her for anything. Paisley was just…irrelevant.

"Regardless of how he reacts, I want the truth." Paisley turned and crossed to the front door. She flicked the closed sign to Open and tugged on the antique doorknob. "I'm not for sale, so unless you're here to plan a wedding to someone else, we're done."

The antique etching on the knob dug into her palm, but she kept her grip tight. Her nerves were shot and she hated how Lucas thought he could manipulate her into some absurd binding commitment.

She stared straight ahead at the wall of mannequins, each draped with an elegant gown. She would not let him win this round. If she had to work to find the truth herself, so be it.

His feet scuffed across the hardwood floor as he drew closer. Lucas stopped just beside her and leaned in. That warm breath of his washed over her collarbone, her neck, sending shivers up her arms she couldn't afford to relish.

"When you come to your senses, you know where to find me."

She closed her eyes as he walked by, and attempted to hold her breath so she didn't have to inhale that sexy scent of his. But, even after he was gone, his presence lingered. A powerful man like Lucas knew how to make an impact without saying a word.

But she'd gone to him initially, so she had no one to blame but herself for awakening the beast.

Still, taking the risk had been necessary because there was no one to tell her the truth and Paisley deserved to know who her father was. It wasn't like she could just march into the jail and demand Sterling tell her what he knew…if he even knew anything to begin with.

Lucas was the best P.I. He would and she believed could find the truth so the benefit of the outcome would far outweigh the pain of marrying the only man she'd ever loved and lost.

Blowing out a sigh, Paisley moved through her bridal boutique and headed for her white antique desk toward the back. She often did consultations here, but today she needed to check her emails and make sure her incoming orders were on time. Timing was everything in this business with jittery brides and deadlines.

Paisley took a seat at her desk and pulled up her messages on her laptop. The most recent one stopped her heart.

No. This could not be happening.

She read through the email once again, praying she'd read it wrong. Her hands shook as she tried to clasp them in her lap. Tears burned her eyes, and her breath caught in her throat.

The thirty-five-thousand-dollar gown she'd ordered for a bride was now no longer needed. The wedding had been called off and the mother of the bride was refusing to pay the remainder of the fee she'd agreed to pay. She was sure Paisley would understand and could return the gown.

Sure, in theory that sounded great, but in the real world a gown with that price tag couldn't be returned like a pair of shoes.

Paisley didn't know if she wanted to just sit there and cry or throw a tantrum. Her eyes darted to the minibar she kept for brides and their guests. Mimosas for morning guests and rosé for the afternoon and evening crowd. Paisley had never indulged while at work, but today was proving to be worthy of a good buzz.

Once she got home, she'd open the bottle of Reisling she'd been saving for a special occasion; after all, she'd given up on something special actually happening.

Slouching back in her seat, Paisley wondered how she'd ever recover from not only the Sterling debacle, but now the major setback with the gown that she would be stuck with. A gown that cost more than her car. A blow like this could absolutely destroy her business and her livelihood.

Dread curled low in her belly. There was a temporary answer to her problems. She just didn't want to admit it even to herself.

But at this point, she didn't have much of a choice. She was going to have to marry Lucas Ford.

# Three

Sterling Perry sank on the edge of his cot and rested his elbows on his knees. This was no way for a man of his standing to live. He was Sterling Perry, damn it. When he spoke, people snapped to attention and obeyed his every command.

Whoever the hell had framed him would regret the day they ever crossed him. This was no accident. Someone outside these prison walls knew the truth and they'd yet to come forward. He wasn't a damn murderer.

But here he sat, still in this blasted cell,

all because he'd made a few minor mistakes and then a body had been found at one of his construction sites once the floodwaters receded. The body hadn't even been identified, so how the hell did they even have a motive to pin all of this on him?

Sterling had been locked up too damn long, having been denied bail. According to the powers that be, they considered him a flight risk.

Bullshit. He wasn't going anywhere, except maybe to see his son, Roarke. One would think a crusading attorney son would come to his father's defense, but not Roarke.

What the hell did a man have to do to earn a little respect?

According to his attorney, there was another chance to petition for bail coming up. Sterling needed out of this place and he needed to get back to the Texas Cattleman's Club because he sure as hell had every intention of becoming the president of the newest chapter.

Sterling came to his feet and blew out a sigh. He wouldn't be in here forever and the time he'd spent so far had only got his gut churning and mind rolling. Roarke had never approved of Sterling's business dealings, so it shouldn't come as a surprise that he hadn't come to his father's aide.

But was he even Roarke's father? Because Sterling had some serious doubts about his late wife's fidelity.

Maybe there was a way to get that rumor out there without sounding like a jaded husband. Shouldn't Roarke know the truth? There was that period where Sterling's wife had been sneaky, distant. He'd always suspected an affair.

He wouldn't be surprised one bit if Roarke was a love child.

Sterling couldn't help the smile that spread across his face. Soon. Very soon people would know just how powerful and mighty Sterling Perry truly was. If they thought he was a shark before, they'd better watch out. Even these bars couldn't hold him back.

The murderer needed to be found, and Sterling needed to secure his position at the club and find the truth about Roarke. There was too much to do and he had run out of patience.

Lucas didn't even try to hide the smile as he waited for the penthouse elevator to slide open the next morning. The security guard for his building had already notified Lucas of the petite blonde heading his way…and according to Nyle, she didn't look too happy.

All the more reason for him to celebrate. If Paisley was here and in a bad mood, that could only mean one thing. Wedding bells would be ringing soon.

Lucas hooked his thumbs on his belt loops and whistled. "Here Comes the Bride" seemed appropriate, but there was no need to completely piss her off so he went with an old country song instead.

The door whooshed open and Paisley stepped into his penthouse. That narrowed gaze and set jaw said more than any words could. Yes, definitely not the time for "Here Comes the Bride."

"Beautiful morning for a visit," he called out to her.

Paisley shot him a glare and Lucas bit the inside of his cheek to keep from laughing. He hadn't been out at all, but the sunshine beamed through his wall of windows.

"Stop looking so damn smug," she stated, marching farther into his penthouse. "This is not going to go the way you think."

As she brushed past him as if she had every right to barge into his home, Lucas chuckled. Oh, he had every intention of getting exactly what he wanted—Paisley in his bed and her having his child. That didn't seem like a high price to pay for all he would be doing for her.

Lucas spun on his heel and followed those swaying hips into the living area.

"First of all," she started, spinning around with her finger pointed right at him like a dagger, "we will get married, but make no mistake, this isn't some happy-ever-after. Don't think that I love you or I have some fantasy that this will be some fairy tale."

Love and fairy tale? No, none of that had entered his mind. What did love have to do with marriage? Thankfully, she knew exactly what this was and wasn't.

Well, there was one thing she didn't know, but he'd save the heir talk for a bit later. He had her here now and he needed to keep her since he was making headway.

"Any other stipulations?" he asked her.

Lucas felt it best to just let her think she called the shots. So long as he got what he wanted out of the deal, he didn't care what she thought.

He wanted a child of his own and justice against Sterling Perry. And Paisley could give him both.

"I want a prenup and everything we agree on in writing," she added. "There will be no surprises at the end of our marriage and my business will not suffer."

Lucas couldn't help but admire her for putting their past, and her emotions, aside to keep her dream alive. He had his own dreams, but they were quite different from hers.

"What brought you here now?" he asked, crossing his arms over his chest and leveling her gaze.

"There was a…minor setback at the boutique." She fidgeted with the strap of her bag resting on her forearm. "I just realized that I can't do it alone and as much as I hate being here, I'm not going to let my business fall simply because my pride got in the way."

Another notch up on the scale of admiration. Maybe she had changed from the girl who had been too afraid to face their difficulties head-on.

Regardless, they were different people

now and nothing about their past played a role in this situation. He wasn't the same naive boy he was back then, young and in love—or what he thought was love. Lucas had a lucrative business and while he might not believe in love in the terms of marriage, he did believe in love of family and he wanted one of his own. He wanted to have that security of passing a legacy down to his children.

Lucas dropped his hands to his sides and closed the space between them. As he grew closer, Paisley tipped her head back to stare up at him and that perfect mix of colors in her eyes never failed to punch him in the gut with lust.

Lust he could handle; in fact, he welcomed it. Having Paisely again wouldn't be a hardship.

"Just so I have everything clear for my attorney to draw up the proper papers, you want me to make sure your business is set to continue to prosper, you need me to find out the truth about your father and you want all of this to have an expiration date."

She pursed her lips as her eyes darted away. That slight slip of her resolve had him swelling with the knowledge that she might come off as headstrong, but she still had that underlying vulnerability he remembered.

And that was the damn crux of the situation. He wanted to be the one to save her. Even after the ridiculous way things ended and all the time that had passed, he couldn't deny the ego trip at the fact she'd come to him for help. Which only meant she'd been thinking of him.

At some point, he'd want answers about the past. Not that it would make any difference, nor did he want to relive everything, but he did wonder. And that bit about his dad going to her? Lucas wasn't so sure that was the whole truth.

"Are you even going to ask what I want out of this?" Lucas couldn't stop himself. He reached out and trailed his fingertip down her creamy cheek and along her jaw-line. "Or are you just going to trust me?"

She licked her lips as she continued to stare. "I…um. I assume you'll tell me."

Easing his thumb over her moist bottom lip, he smiled. "I want you in my bed. For as long as we're married, we will be man and wife in every way. There's no way I can live with you and not touch you, not want you. Not have you all to myself."

Paisley's eyes widened as she gasped. "You know I'm not staying forever. Why would you want to pretend this is real?"

Lucas was done playing games. He framed her face with both hands and cov-ered her mouth. The bag she had on her arm bumped his abdomen, then fell with a thud to the floor.

Paisley let out a little squeak as he all but consumed her. She opened for him, just as she always had. Some things never changed. She'd never hesitated with her re-sponse to him and now was no different. She gripped his biceps as if she needed to hold on or hold him in place—either way was fine with him.

Damn. She tasted just as sweet as he remembered. Lucas threaded his fingers through her hair and tipped her head back. Paisley arched against him as he nipped at her lips and slowly pulled away.

"Was that you pretending?" he asked, his voice surprisingly stronger than he actually felt. "Because I just want to make sure I don't get confused about what's real or pretend."

Paisley took a step back, then another, until she bumped into the curved staircase. Her shaky hand went to her lips and she closed her eyes.

Lucas was having a bit of a problem keeping himself in check. He wanted nothing more than to strip her bare and take her right here in his living room. But that was how they'd been when they were younger. They'd been all over each other. Young love had carried them so far, but ultimately, not far enough.

Still, having her in his home stirred something primal in him and he was positive he didn't want her leaving. Call him selfish, but he wanted Paisley and he wanted her right here.

"Chemistry doesn't mean anything," she retorted.

If there had been any conviction in her tone, he might believe her. If she hadn't arched that sweet, curvy body against his, he might think she didn't want more. But he knew better. She'd come to him, pride aside.

She could have chosen anyone else to help her, but she wanted him. Despite everything that happened in their past, they still had a bond and he knew she trusted him with her case.

Lucas reached for her, sliding his hand across her cheek and up into her hair. "You want to end the marriage, I get that. Do you have an expiration date?"

Those hazel eyes never wavered from his. "If Sterling turns out to be my father and recognizes me, then I want out. I don't want someone to take care of me forever. I want to stand on my own. But I'm not stupid enough to ignore the fact that I need help, because I won't let my business suffer. It's all I have left."

So, it all came down to money. Most things in life did, he realized. Plus, he understood the need to protect something you'd built. Wasn't that the reason he wanted a child to pass his business down to? All she wanted was to keep her shop running and live comfortably—which she could right here in his penthouse.

"Fine." Lucas leaned down, brushed his lips over hers once more before stepping back. "You will be in my bed every night. Nonnegotiable. We'll marry in Vegas, have our honeymoon and I'll get to the bottom of the letter about your father."

"Vegas?" she asked, quirking a brow. "That doesn't sound like you."

"It's fast, simple." Lucas smiled. "Unless you wanted to prepare and plan. A cathedral wedding would be fine, and actually not bad for my reputation. We could invite the press and—"

"Vegas it is." She narrowed her eyes. "One more stipulation. You're buying the gown of my choosing."

Lucas could care less about the gown—more what was beneath. He'd have something sexy and sheer ordered for her for their wedding night and have it waiting in their suite.

He'd also have his jeweler get a stunning rock sent over as soon as possible. Their marriage might not be traditional, but Lucas wasn't going to have his wife walking around with anything less than the best.

"Done," he finally agreed.

Paisley stared at him another minute, cautiously keeping her emotions guarded, which he didn't like. The Paisley he used to know had always been an open book, and she kept slipping into that state, but he could also see the independent woman she'd worked so hard to become. She was strong, she was resilient…and she was his.

Finally.

She'd have his ring on her finger and her body in his bed. This might not be the way he'd imagined they'd end up together, but they were going to be together nonetheless. They'd both get what they wanted.

Lucas had been naive years ago to think love would carry them through all their happy days and into old age. Then life smacked him in the face with a dose of reality and he finally saw that love didn't exist. Money, power, careers—those things lasted and could be controlled. Love was nothing but a made-up emotion for people who lived in a fantasy world.

Love wasn't for him…and never would be.

# Four

*They still hadn't discovered it was me. Sterling Perry was exactly where he needed to be. Oh, he hadn't murdered anyone, but the fact that he was taking the fall for my mistake thrilled me more than I should allow.*

*The man was a dirty bastard and deserved to rot in prison...or hell. Either were appropriate for the selfish, greedy man. He ruined my life, ruined so many others. The town and TCC were better off without him.*

*So long as he stayed in prison and the body wasn't identified, I'd be home free. I'd already lost so much, I deserved happiness and that was exactly what I'd be going after...no matter who I had to step on or over to get there.*

*Ryder Currin was another who'd ruined my life, but he'd pay, too. He deserved no less than the treatment Sterling was getting. They'd both pay, maybe in different ways, but they'd pay.*

*People would remember me for great things, not the murder that I was forced to commit. I'd had no choice! My hands had been tied and then I'd panicked. But then my plans had fallen into place. I will ultimately come out on top. You wait and see.*

*My future will be secure and everyone will know my name.*

*I promise you that. Wait and see.*

"What the hell is that?"

Paisley glanced down at her one-of-a-kind lace jumpsuit. The plunging neckline, the open back, the slit up the front of the legs to her thigh…they were all sexy, flamboyant and one hundred percent not part of the wedding "gown" of her dreams.

Which was why she'd purchased the tacky ensemble—with Lucas's credit card, of course. The nude swatches of material were strategically placed beneath the lace, but the rest was bare skin.

Oh, the look on his face was priceless and worth every bit of nerves she had curling in her belly.

Mustering up all the confidence and attitude, Paisley held her hands out wide and gave a dramatic turn. "You like? I figured since we're in Vegas, I might as well have some fun. But I wanted to be sexy for my fiancé."

His eyes raked over her and that visual sampling he gave had her trembling. This wasn't supposed to arouse her. She wanted to torment him. Damn him and those baby blues she never could ignore.

"Every damn person can see through that," he growled.

Lucas grabbed her arm and ushered her to the nearest nook at the Hunka-Hunka Burnin' Love Chapel. Despite the name, this was the classiest chapel on the strip and Lucas had paid to have the absolute best. He also paid for them to have the place to themselves, save for the man marrying them and a couple witnesses.

"This isn't like you," he stated, backing her into a corner.

Paisley placed her hands on his firm chest and stared up at him. "Marrying for anything less than love isn't like me, either, yet here we are. I think I look damn good, thank you for noticing."

Lucas placed a hand on either side of her face, caging her in even more. With her own hands trapped between their bodies, Paisley tried her hardest not to curl her fingers into him in an instinctive attempt to feel more.

His rich, masculine scent enveloped her

just the same as if he fully wrapped his arms around her body. The man exuded power without saying a word and Paisley knew if she didn't keep her mind sharp and her heart guarded, she'd find herself falling for him once again.

And she wasn't so sure she'd ever fallen out of love to begin with. Leaving him certainly hadn't been her idea, but her hands had been tied and as much as the move had hurt, she'd known Lucas had needed to get away from her to achieve his goals.

Wasn't that the old saying? If you love something set it free? Well, she'd done exactly that and look how all of that turned out. She was in Vegas in the tackiest outfit she could find, ready to sell her soul.

Lucas leaned in closer, and his warm breath tickled the side of her neck at the same time he trailed his fingertip down the low V of her dress between her breasts. Shivers raced through her and there was no way she could ignore the trembling. Her body was clearly betraying her when all she wanted was to stay in charge. So much for that.

"My little conservative minx." He trailed his lips over her neck, traveling from one side to the other. "You think I'm upset about this? You're mine, Tart. Let anyone look, but I'll be the one touching you, pleasuring you."

Paisley closed her eyes, unable to stop the visual images from rolling through her mind. Lucas continued feathering that fingertip across her heated skin, and she cursed herself for playing games. She should've shown up in something with a high neck and full sleeves. But no, she'd wanted tacky, yet sexy as hell just to be spiteful.

"If we're done playing games, let's go make this legal."

Before Paisley could take a breath, Lucas covered her mouth with his. His body pressed hers against the wall, and she barely had time to register the glorious contact before her body arched to his and he slid his hands up her bare arms. He curled his fingers around her shoulders and urged her even closer.

The power from his touch, his strength, had her knees going weak, but the way he kissed her…there were no words. There was something passionate, hot, yet gentle about him.

Lucas slid his lips gently across hers before easing back.

"Just wanted to practice the whole kiss-the-bride part," he said with a smirk. "You ready to become Mrs. Lucas Ford?"

Ready? Now that she was here, Paisley worried she'd gotten in over her head. But despite everything, she trusted him to find the truth.

Paisley smiled wide and patted his cheek, ignoring her thumping heart from that heated kiss. "I'll keep my own name, but thanks for the offer."

The woman was going to be the death of him. If she didn't kill him with that smart mouth, that damn svelte body wrapped in lace would surely do the trick. The only parts of her flesh he couldn't see were the areas a skimpy bikini would cover.

Paisley had the ability to order any wedding gown in the world and she'd chosen the most ridiculous, sexiest jumpsuit. Damn it if he wasn't even more aroused and intrigued at her snarky act. At least this wouldn't be a boring marriage.

He was counting on her being just as fiery in bed.

"You may now kiss your bride."

At the officiant's word, Lucas circled her waist with his hands and pulled her hips to his, instantly capturing her lips. Much like moments ago in the hallway, Paisley melted against him. She had always been a passionate woman and now he was going to get to experience that all over again.

Paisley broke the kiss and flattened her hands on his chest. "I think that covers it," she stated with a breathless sigh. "I'll take a nice bottle of prosecco in my suite, please."

Lucas dug his fingertips into the dip in her waist. "We've barely begun," he murmured. "And it's not your suite. It's ours."

Paisley pulled away and smiled over gritted teeth. "I'm ready to get to *our* suite and relax."

Lucas shot a wink to the officiant. "The honeymoon can't start too early."

Paisley twisted out of his grasp and turned to go back down the short, narrow aisle. Lucas nodded to the witnesses and turned to follow his bride. Never in his wildest dreams—and he'd had some wild ones—did he ever think he'd marry Paisley or have the woman standing in practically nothing as he slid a band of diamonds onto her finger.

Speaking of, Paisley hadn't reacted one bit when he'd put that ten-carat flawless diamond on her finger when they'd taken off from Houston. In fact, she'd stared out the window and barely said a word to him.

Maybe he shouldn't have gone for something so traditional. Someone like Paisley would want an emerald or a ruby. He should—

No. Hell, no. What was he thinking? He wasn't getting her something else. Between the engagement ring and now the wedding band, she had enough on that finger to help support her shop. This wasn't for love or until death did they part. Paisley already had an expiration date on their marriage.

Of course, if she produced an heir, there was no way he'd divorce her. He didn't just want her in his bed, he wanted her to give him a child. Paisley had always wanted children, or she used to when they were together before. They'd often dreamed of one day having their own family.

Lucas slipped his arm around her waist and guided her out to the waiting car. As soon as he settled in beside her and the driver closed the door, Paisley turned to face him.

"I sent a copy of my mother's letter to

your email," she started. "When we get back to the room, we can start digging into that and you can share what you've discovered so far. I can answer questions about my mom's past, but—"

Lucas leaned over and covered her mouth with his. He shifted so that he pressed her against the back of the leather seat as the driver took them down the Strip. Lights from the hotels flashed through the windows, but nothing else mattered except the fact that his new bride instantly wanted to get down to business.

Well, he did, too, but a completely different kind.

Paisley shoved against his chest and turned her head away. "Can you focus?"

Lucas curved his hand around her upper thigh and gave a slight squeeze. "Oh, I'm plenty focused."

Those hazel eyes with flecks of emerald landed on him. "You promised to help find the truth and I want to be part of that process."

He stroked the inside of her thigh with his thumb. "You're my wife now. You'll be part of everything."

Her brows shot up. "I thought you'd try to exclude me."

"I see no reason in leaving you out when this is your life I'm dealing with."

Clearly his response shocked her. She shook her head and glanced out the window as the car turned into the front of their hotel.

"I'll never understand you," she murmured.

Lucas didn't bother hiding his smile. He was banking on her being kept off guard. He wanted her wondering what he'd do next. Pretty much like she had always done to him, and today with that damn lace number was no exception.

That was just one of the things he'd always loved about her—her ability to keep him on his toes. The way she'd challenged him and always had him guessing what she'd do next had made for a great relationship…until the ultimate moment when she'd caught him off guard and destroyed his heart.

"How much did this scrap of lace cost me?" he asked.

The car came to a stop and Paisley turned to him with a smile on her face. "I don't recall, but it was worth every penny. Wouldn't you agree?"

Her door opened before he could answer and the driver extended his hand to assist Paisley. Lucas went out into the night after her and nodded his thanks to their chauffer.

As he and his bride waltzed through the spacious five-story lobby, she got some looks. Not because of the nearly sheer getup—this was Vegas, after all—but because she was so damn stunning that she could've been wearing a sack and she still would've drawn attention.

As they approached the elevators, Lucas settled his hand on the small of her bare back and swiped his card that would take them to the VIP floors. They weren't staying in a traditional honeymoon suite, but the nicest high-roller penthouse available. The three-thousand-square-foot room complete with their own waitstaff was ready and waiting for them.

Lucas would immediately dismiss the staff and have them on standby should he and Paisley need more food and wine. Other than that, he fully planned on keeping his wife all to himself tonight.

No way in hell were they going to worry about Sterling Perry or her mother or some damn letter.

Lucas had just one concern: How the hell did he get that lace jumpsuit off?

# Five

Paisley's hands shook as she stared at the enormous bathroom in their suite. Her entire apartment could fit in here and there would still be extra space.

The heated marble floors, the open shower big enough for a party, the wall of mirrors and the chandelier with so many twinkling lights…there was just so much to take in and she didn't even want to know what this place cost per night.

She also knew Lucas wasn't ready to dive into the letter or the truth. He was ready to dive into her pants. Paisley wasn't even going to pretend she wasn't looking forward to feeling his body against her again. She was human; she had basic needs.

But there was nothing basic about what she and Lucas had once shared. He'd always been an attentive lover, but they'd been so young. Clearly they'd both changed over the years.

Paisley took a step back and glanced at herself in the floor-length mirror. She certainly didn't have the same body she'd once had. Gravity and doughnuts had made a few alterations.

Might as well get out of this ridiculous outfit. She'd been in such a spiteful mood when she'd gone wedding dress shopping for herself. Of course she had her favorites. There was one magnificent gown she'd had her eye on for the past few months.

Like any woman, especially one owning a bridal boutique, Paisley had her own vision of her big day. But there was no way in hell she was wasting any of that fairy-tale stuff on Lucas. Because one day she would marry for love. She'd get that gown of her dreams, the sparkling accessories, her mother's simple diamond necklace, maybe even plan a destination wedding or a grand cathedral ceremony. Or maybe she'd go with a classy garden wedding.

None of those daydreams mattered now. All that mattered was trying to get through her current marriage with her heart still intact and finding the truth about her father.

She honestly didn't know if she wanted Sterling to be her biological dad or not. He'd destroyed her finances, not to mention that of others, and he was just an evil, spiteful man. He currently sat in a jail cell, after being denied bail, because he was accused of fraud and not too long ago a body had been found on one of his work sites.

The thought sent a shudder through her. No, that was not the type of man she wanted for a father.

On the other hand, knowing who and where she came from would at least give her a sense of belonging. She certainly felt a yawning void since her mother's passing. There was an emptiness in her life she hadn't expected, and a large part of her seemed to just be going through the daily motions. The sense of being lost and floating along seemed to grow worse. Her heart ached and she was so utterly confused she truly had no clue what to do next.

Marrying Lucas didn't help.

He'd had her suitcase brought up to the suite before the ceremony. Paisley had changed at the chapel so she could surprise her husband. Mission accomplished.

Paisley had brought her robe into the bathroom a few minutes ago and hung it on the back of the hook next to the garden tub. She had no clue what to expect when she stepped out, but she was thankful he was giving her a few minutes of space.

The tap on the door pulled her from her thoughts. There went that alone time.

"You plan on hiding much longer?" Lucas called through the double doors.

Paisley sighed as she straightened and reached around her neck for the hidden closure. "Almost done."

The doors opened just as her top fell to her waist. Lucas's vibrant eyes zeroed in on her bare breasts as he remained in the doorway. Paisley didn't bother covering herself. He might as well see that she wasn't a stick-thin twenty-year-old like she used to be.

From the clenched jaw and tight lips, he wasn't disappointed in her curves. That fact not only boosted her confidence, but sent a shiver of arousal through her. She hadn't cared what he thought about her until just this minute. Which was silly because she was happy with her body and wouldn't change for any man.

"I knew that getup looked like you were wearing nothing beneath," he stated. "But you sure as hell were bare."

Paisley smiled. Feeling extra saucy, she slid her thumbs into the material gathered at her waist and shoved it on down to pool at her feet. Carefully, she stepped out of the garment, leaving her standing before him in only her spiked, strappy heels.

He'd already shed his jacket and tie and loosened the top button on his black shirt. His hair was rumpled from his Stetson, his sleeves were rolled up onto muscular forearms, and judging by the way he looked at her, it would be a miracle if they didn't set this place on fire just from the electricity charging between them.

Chemistry…they still had it. Quite possibly even stronger than their first time around.

Regardless of the circumstances surrounding their marriage, there was no denying their attraction and there was no use fighting it. Paisley wondered if she needed time to grasp their new, temporary reality, but all she needed was that boost of courage that only came from one of Lucas's sexy stares.

"Had I known what you weren't wearing, we would've taken the long way here from the chapel." Lucas stalked toward her, unbuttoning his shirt and discarding it across the floor. "Do you even know how sexy you are? More than I remember."

Did that mean he'd thought about her over the years? Paisley wasn't about to admit she'd done her fair share of fantasizing. She was stronger now, more independent...or trying like hell to be. The blows she'd been delivered lately had forced her to admit vulnerability. She hated needing anybody, but there was also no need in being stupid about her situation. She needed Lucas now, in more than one way. He'd always been her weakness.

Before he could touch her, Paisley put her hands on his bare chest and looked up at him. "This can't be more than, well...this."

His brows drew in. "What?"

"Sex. This marriage isn't more than you helping me and sex. I can't get hurt, Lucas."

His fingertips trailed over her hips, into the dip of her waist and over the sides of her breasts. All the while he kept his gaze locked firmly on hers.

"You think I'd hurt you?"

He took one step, closing the last bit of distance between them. With a quick, expert move, Lucas reached for her hands, pulled them down to her sides and gently behind her back. With one firm grip, he secured her wrists and towered over her.

With his free hand, he covered her neck and stroked his thumb along the sensitive spot behind her ear, and then he ran a fingertip over her lips.

"I'd never hurt you," he murmured. "But I'm keeping myself guarded as well since you were the one who broke my heart with a letter and a vanishing act."

He gave her no chance to defend herself as his hand disappeared, quickly replaced by his mouth.

Paisley had no choice but to arch against him in this current situation. He had complete and utter control and the very female, aching, needy part of her wanted him to do whatever he planned. She trusted him completely with her body. It was her heart that she had to keep protected.

At least they were both in agreement that their hearts had no place in this marriage. Now, if she could just remember that as they went through the rest of their days as husband and wife while playing house.

Paisley opened to him, welcoming the passion. There was something so familiar, yet so strangely new with having Lucas consume her. That young adult body had turned into manly muscle and the sometimes timid touch was now all demanding. A man who knew what he wanted, and who he wanted, was so damn sexy.

There was no question that Lucas had every intention of remaining dominant and maybe, just in the case of the bedroom, she'd let go of the reins for now. She found his strength and power arousing and refreshing from guys she'd dated in the past.

Paisley looped her arms around his neck, threading her fingers through his thick hair. Was it naive of her to want to get lost in him for just a bit? This was no typical wedding night, but that didn't mean she wouldn't thoroughly enjoy herself and the man she now called her husband.

Lucas lifted her and walked to the vanity. The cool marble against her heated skin had Paisley shivering, but that shock was nothing compared to the man standing between her spread legs looking like he wanted to devour her.

With his heavy-lidded eyes homing in on her, Lucas took one step back to rid himself of all his clothes. He stood completely bare before her, a sight she never thought she'd see again, let alone in this instance. Lucas Ford was her husband and she had a very real feeling that someone was not going to come out the other side unscathed.

"Stay with me, Tart."

His husky words pulled her back. She didn't want to be anywhere else. She didn't want to worry about tomorrow or even next month. She only wanted this moment with

Lucas…the way it should've been so many years ago.

She reached for him. "I'm right here."

Lucas lifted her legs by gripping the back of her thighs and eased her to the edge of the counter. Paisley clung to his shoulders in anticipation.

"Protection?" she asked.

Those baby blues traveled from between their bodies up to her face. "I want to feel my wife. Are you worried? I've always used something, except with you."

When they'd been younger and so lost in each other they'd forgotten a couple of times. She wagered a mental battle with herself, but ultimately knew what she wanted.

"You're the only man I've ever been with that way."

Lucas's eyes darkened as he pulled her hips closer and finally joined their bodies. Paisley closed her eyes, wanting to hold on to every single sensation and freeze this moment.

So much for guarding her emotions.

"Look at me," he demanded.

The second she locked her gaze with his, Lucas began to move. The tips of his fingers dug into her hips and she tipped her pelvis just so, enough to create the most pleasurable experience for both of them.

There was something so intimate about staring at Lucas, something she couldn't put her finger on. But she didn't want to look away. The man held her captivated as he continued to pump his hips. He reached between them and touched her at the spot she ached most.

Paisley cried out as a wave of pleasure crashed into her. Her head dropped back as she squeezed her eyes shut. A second later, Lucas's hands framed her face and tipped her head back up to meet his demanding kiss.

Her body continued to spiral out of control as he claimed more and more from her. There was nothing outside these walls. No secrets, no worries. Everything that mattered was right here, raw and abandoned. Real emotions they couldn't hide.

The moment Paisley's shivers ceased, she pulled from the kiss and glanced up to Lucas. He looked down at her, hunger in his eyes and the muscles in his jaw clenched.

Paisley smiled as she leaned back on her elbows and locked her ankles behind his back. The act of relinquishing total control had Lucas flattening a hand on her abdomen as he pumped harder, faster.

When he trembled, Paisley became utterly captivated as his climax consumed him. She kept her eyes locked onto his and Lucas didn't look away, which only turned her on even more.

The man was demanding, cocky, arrogant...even during sex.

Why did that all have to be so damn arousing? She'd already been pleasured, yet she wasn't quite ready to give up this warmth, this passion.

Once he calmed, Lucas reached down and

cupped both of her breasts. Paisley waited, wondering what he'd say or do next. When the silence became too much, she finally eased all the way up and dropped her legs to rub against the sides of his.

"If you only wanted sex from this marriage, I'd say we're off to a hell of a start," she told him, trying to maintain her nonchalant image.

Lucas leaned down and captured her lips for a short, hot kiss that had her toes curling. Then he eased back and gave her that naughty grin she'd never forgotten.

"Sex is a given," he retorted. "But I want a child. Our child."

# Six

Maybe now wasn't the best time to make that announcement. Lucas should've carried her into the grand bedroom with a wall of one-way windows overlooking the Strip. He should've taken his time with her, laid her out on the bed and showed her exactly what they'd missed from their years apart.

But better she knew what she was getting into. Better she knew why he married her...or at least part of the reason. Paisley didn't need to be informed of the whole revenge scheme he'd thought of if Sterling turned out to be her biological father.

"A baby?" she repeated, her tone leaving no question as to her irritation. "You married me thinking I'd be... What? Your ticket to fatherhood? Isn't this something you should've mentioned before we said 'I do'?"

She pushed off the counter and edged around him to the silky red robe she'd hung near the tub big enough for a party. He watched as she jerked the lapels closed and knotted the belt at her waist.

Figuring he should put on something, Lucas grabbed his black boxer briefs and stepped into them.

"I knew you wanted something from me," she muttered as she pulled her hair from the robe, sending the tousled strands down over her shoulders. "I should've been more selective on who I asked help from. This is..."

She shook her head and raked her hands

through her hair. Lucas crossed his arms over his chest.

"I didn't mean I wanted you to give me a child now," he told her. "I do want a child, someone I can pass my company down to. Neither of us is looking for love, but there's no reason we can't get what we want."

Her mouth dropped open as her brows shot up. "Do you hear yourself? I asked you to find the truth about my father. You're asking me to give you a human being. One of those will bind us together for life. Is that what you want with me?"

"I don't believe in love, so finding someone to share my heart isn't an option. Children are family and that's a whole other aspect of feelings and one I am open to." He took a step toward her, but stopped when she put her hands up. "We always discussed children. Remember?"

"I remember," she stated, dropping her hands to her sides. "I also remember that we were in love at the time and had unrealistic expectations on life and our future. This isn't some young lover's dream, Lucas. You can't just bring a baby into the world because you want someone to take your business. That's…that's…archaic."

Lucas wasn't about to get into an argument on his wedding night—regardless of the fact this wasn't a typical wedding or marriage. The last thing he wanted was too much conflict at this early stage.

"We can discuss this later." He reached down and gathered his clothes, then scooped up her lace jumpsuit. "For the rest of this weekend, can't we just enjoy the honeymoon?"

The way she stood there with that messy, sexy hair, those killer heels and that silky robe made Lucas want to throw her over his shoulder and march right into the bedroom for round two.

Hmm…was that archaic as well?

If she knew he was using her as a way to seek revenge on Sterling, she'd sure as hell never agree to a child. The ground he treaded on was shaky at best and each step he took could be fatal to his plan.

"You get this weekend," she told him. "And then we're getting to the bottom of Sterling and my mother and whatever history they had."

Surprised she gave in, Lucas nodded. "I'll make Sterling my top priority."

Because if Sterling was indeed Paisley's father, Lucas had every intention of letting his new father-in-law know just who was in charge and who ultimately would come out on top.

Lucas stared up at the neon sign attached to the dingy bar Paisley's mother used to work at decades ago. Just because the place still existed didn't mean anyone would remember Lynette Morgan.

But he had to start somewhere other than a cryptic letter so here he was. He often put his best men on the grunt work of the jobs they took on, but this case was too personal. Besides, Lucas liked getting back to the basics of his business.

The second Lucas tugged open the heavy door, loud country music from a live band spilled out. Couples danced on the scarred wood floor and the long bar that stretched from front to back was actually pretty crowded. Obviously there was a reason this place had stayed in business so long. He'd found the dive places were usually the hidden gems when it came to bars and restaurants.

Lucas eased his way toward the bar and zeroed in on the older bartender at the end. From the looks of the younger staff, that would be the only person in this place who might remember anything at all.

As he eased through a crowd of women who should be cut off their spirits, Lucas slid a photo from his pocket and rounded the edge of the bar. When the bartender glanced his way, Lucas waved a hand.

"What can I get ya?" the man yelled over the band.

Lucas flipped the picture up. "You recognize this woman?"

The bartender narrowed his gaze and leaned forward, then nodded. "Lynette. I remember her. Hated to hear of her passing. Damn shame."

Yes, it was. Lucas wished like hell Paisley hadn't lost her mother. To make matters worse, a complete bastard might turn out to be her father. Even so, Lucas couldn't let guilt and tragedy stop him from seeking revenge. Sterling had destroyed Lucas's father and it was time for him to pay.

"When she worked here, did she have any guys that hung around or anyone she mentioned dating?"

He hated yelling over this crowd, but he and Paisley had gotten home from Vegas a couple hours ago and he wanted to get this ball rolling. He figured a Monday night wouldn't be too crowded, but apparently this was half off wing night.

He'd chosen to come straight here for one because he wanted to dive straight in, but he also needed space to think. The damn woman was driving him out of his mind with want, lust, need. He didn't recall needing anyone the way he'd found himself craving her the past few days, not even when they were together the first time.

They'd spent their honeymoon in the suite, completely naked, save for the few times she'd thrown on his shirt when they'd had carpet picnics. They'd even made love on his private jet on their way home.

So, yeah. The chemistry was stronger than ever.

"There was an older man that came around," the bartender stated, pulling Lucas back into the moment. "Wealthy. Don't know his name, but he always wore a suit and tossed out hundred dollar bills for tips. Always thought the guy was arrogant."

Buster's Bar was certainly not the type of establishment you'd toss around wads of cash. That type of cockiness sounded like Sterling Perry, but this definitely wasn't enough proof to confront the guy.

"Would you know his name if you heard it?" Lucas prompted.

"I never heard Lynette say," the old guy replied. "But she sure was smitten with whoever it was."

Lucas nodded and shoved the photo back into his pocket. He pulled out another and held it up.

"Do you recognize this man?"

The man's eyes narrowed and he thought for a moment. "It's been a long time, but I don't think I've seen him before."

Lucas gritted his teeth against the frustration and offered a smile. "Thanks for your time."

"Can I get you a beer?"

Lucas offered a smile. "Next time," he promised. He figured he'd bring Paisley back sometime. There might be more questions once he dug a little deeper.

He weaved his way back through the crowd and out into the night. Just being away from his wife for an hour had him itching to get home. Yes, he'd needed a few minutes to himself, but now he realized he wanted to be with her. Their time in Vegas had been intense, but too short. Lucas wanted to schedule another getaway for them soon. First, though, he'd have to find the truth about Sterling.

Maybe this wasn't a traditional marriage, maybe Paisley wanted an end date, but he was taking full advantage of being married to the one woman he'd always wanted. She'd gotten away once, but he had no intention of letting her go again. His reasons were just a tad different this time.

Before, when he'd been young and too trusting, Lucas had been expecting them to live forever after on love and happiness. Now they could live on determination and passion. Hey, that was more than most relationships, right?

He wasn't under some delusion that he'd ever marry for love. Such a notion was for fairy tales and fiction novels. He did want a child and he hadn't lied when he told Paisley he wanted her to be the mother. There'd been no other woman that had filled that bill so the whole fatherhood thing was something he'd thought had been off in the future. But then she'd walked through his office door and the opportunity had landed in his lap.

By the time he got home, Lucas was more than eager to see Paisley. The topic of the baby hadn't been brought up again, but he knew full well she wasn't done. It was something they needed to discuss and he'd much rather talk about a child than the revenge she knew nothing about.

For now, there was no reason for her to think anything other than the fact he was helping her business and they should start a family.

When he stepped off the private elevator, he froze.

What the hell?

Lucas dropped his keys onto the accent table to his right without even looking away from the newly decorated living area. This was…not his style. The throw pillows were everywhere. Some had polka dots, some had stripes. There was a tray on the oversize square ottoman that held candles and flowers.

A few new pictures hung on the walls… pictures with quotes that he didn't want to take the time to read. They wouldn't be staying.

"Oh, hey! You're home."

Lucas glanced toward the open kitchen and nearly swallowed his tongue. Paisley paraded through wearing an apron and heels—only an apron and heels—holding a glass of what he presumed to be his favorite bourbon.

"I hope you don't mind I brought a few of my things over." She strutted toward him and held out the tumbler. "I just thought since I'm staying here, you'd want me to be happy and feel at home."

The moment he took the drink, she turned away, giving him the most impressive view of her bare ass and those legs.

"Dinner will be ready in ten minutes if

you want to change," she called over her shoulder.

Lucas tipped back the amber liquid and welcomed the burn. How long had he been gone? And how the hell did she find the time to do all of this?

He followed her to the kitchen and watched in awe as she pulled something from the oven that smelled better than anything he'd ever created here.

"I hope you like chicken Cordon Bleu." She set the pan on the stove and closed the oven door then reached up to turn off the heat. "There's also an apricot and feta salad to start."

Lucas crossed his arms over his chest and leaned against the counter next to her. "Are you going to just pretend like you didn't completely redecorate and that you're not cooking dinner completely naked?"

She shot him a half grin that didn't help his growing arousal. Damn, she was playing a game. She was playing *him*.

"First of all, I'm not completely naked."

She had the nerve to pat his cheek before she turned back to dinner. "Second, with your archaic way of thinking, I just assumed you'd want me naked in the kitchen. Was I wrong? I'm just trying to be a good wife."

She stopped looking through the cabinets to stare at him, blinking like she was utterly innocent.

Lucas slammed the cabinet door she'd been holding open. In one swift move, he gripped her waist and hoisted her up onto the island behind them. With a squeal, Paisley held on to his shoulders.

"*Innocent* is never a word I would use to describe you." He stepped between her legs and stared directly into her eyes. "Are you done being a smart-ass?"

Paisley shrugged. "Probably not."

"What the hell am I going to do with all of those ruffled pillows on my sofa?"

Paisley laughed. "Admire how much they spruce up the place?"

"They look ridiculous," he grumbled.

Paisley toyed with the button on his shirt. "The honeymoon must really be over if I'm barely wearing anything and you're worried about pillows."

More like he was trying to hold on to the shred of control and not rip her apron off. How could he want her every second of the day? She seemed to have the same feelings, so why was he questioning this?

"Where were you anyway?" she asked, sliding one button undone, then another, and on down she went. "We barely got in the door and you took off."

"Because when we're alone all I want to do is get you on your back," he growled, jerking his shirt off and flinging it to the floor. "I had work to do."

She stilled. "About Sterling?"

Lucas took a step back. "Yeah. I went to the bar your mom worked at during the time she got pregnant with you."

"It's still there?" she asked. "I never go to that side of town, so I never thought about it. Was it all run-down?"

"It's not the best part of town, so it matches the rest of the old buildings," he agreed. "But the bartender remembered your mom."

Paisley hopped off the counter, eyes wide. "What did he say?"

"He knew there was a wealthy man who always hung around, but he didn't know a name."

Paisley pursed her lips and glanced to the floor, her wheels obviously turning. Lucas, on the other hand, had short-circuited the moment she'd waltzed through looking like his every fantasy come to life.

Paisley turned her attention back to him. "I thought everyone knew who Sterling was."

Lucas stepped forward, reaching around to undo the ties at her neck and waist. "Maybe he does know Sterling, but this was a long time ago and he may not have known him then. People change."

The apron fell to the floor between them. Her eyes widened.

"Aren't you hungry?" she asked.

His body stirred. "Starving."

Lucas crushed his mouth to hers, palmed her backside and lifted her against his body as he carried her from the kitchen. Paisley wrapped her legs around him, one of her heels digging into his ass, but he didn't care. He wanted this woman with the snarky mannerisms and quick wit. He wanted her in his bed and he wasn't about to wait another second.

As he stepped into his master suite, her heels clattered to the floor. She threaded her fingers through his hair and groaned.

Those little noises had always gotten him. When they'd been younger, and he'd had considerably less control, those sweet sounds would nearly have him embarrassing himself before they'd even started.

Paisley pulled her lips from his. "Wait," she panted. "I don't want to be just another woman you bring in here. I mean, I know this isn't love or a real marriage, but I just—"

Lucas put his fingertip over her lips. "Clearly I've been with other women since you, but I swear, I've never brought a woman into my bedroom. Ever."

He would stay over at a lover's place, but this was his domain and it never seemed right to have someone invade his space.

Paisley seemed to relax as her lids lowered and she licked her bottom lip.

Every single thing that woman did drove him out of his mind. She'd always held a different spot in his life than any other woman, but he had no clue since she walked back in just how much he'd missed her.

They'd been so damn young before—so clueless.

His eyes were wide-open this time…and his heart completely closed.

They'd been married for three days and they'd barely kept their hands off each other. That was the marriage he wanted with her, the marriage he *needed* with her.

Lucas made quick work of removing his

clothes. The topic of birth control hadn't come up since that first time. He knew she was on something and he'd never deceive her with getting pregnant. He wanted that to be a joint decision…but he would sway her to seeing things his way.

Her hazel eyes raked over him. The way she always seemed to sample him with her eyes made him wonder just how she was going to feel once she discovered his true reason for marrying her.

Guilt had no place in the bedroom or his plan.

Right now all that mattered was that his wife was naked and standing inches from him. He circled her waist with his hands and lifted her onto the bed. With a slight bounce, she laughed and stared up at him with wide eyes.

Lucas rested a knee next to her hip and raked a hand up her thigh, over her flat stomach and on up to circle one pert breast.

Her immediate response to his touch was

definitely one area that hadn't changed. Their connection had always been electrifying and unlike anything he'd ever had with anyone else.

Lucas reached back down, keeping his eyes locked on hers, and gripped the back of her thigh. He settled himself between her legs and thrust into her, earning himself a long, slow moan from his sexy wife.

How the hell was he going to go back to work? He wanted to keep her in his bed and forget all his responsibilities.

When she opened her eyes and stared up at him, Lucas leaned down and covered her mouth. He couldn't look into her eyes, not now. He was confused; he was falling back into their old patterns and forgetting that she'd broken him before. If she started developing feelings, they'd both end up hurt because that was not what all of this was about.

Revenge. That was the key component of his focus.

And the warmth of Paisley. He had to stay in this frame of mind because she took him to a place that he wanted to stay...if only that wasn't some unrealistic fantasy.

Lucas shifted his body fully over hers, dropping her leg and flattening his palms on either side of her head as he lifted slightly. Thankfully her eyes were shut. She arched and tipped her head as she locked her ankles around his back.

Yes. This was what he wanted. Physical connections were something he could most definitely handle, but the emotional ones had no place here.

Paisley curled her fingers around his shoulders, her fingertips digging into his skin. She let out another sultry moan and tightened all around him. Lucas gritted his teeth, following her as his body shuddered and he slipped into a euphoria only Paisley could give him.

He cradled her face with his hands, tucked his head against the crook of her neck and waited until their bodies settled.

Then he rolled to his side, taking her with him, and wondered what the hell he was going to do when she wanted to call this quits.

Because he never wanted to let her go again.

# Seven

"We need proof," Lucas stated as he loaded the dishwasher.

Paisley propped her feet up on the kitchen chair he'd vacated moments ago. She sipped her wine and admired the fine specimen that was her husband. Shirtless, cotton pants hanging low on his narrow hips, hair messed from their lovemaking.

Damn if this wasn't the sexiest thing she'd ever seen. A half-naked man cleaning the kitchen. Yeah, put images like this in a calendar and label it Domestic Men and watch them fly off the shelves. She'd hang one in every room.

"Paisley?"

She blinked and set her glass on the table. "I'm listening."

His brows drew in. "You're staring and I'm starting to feel like a piece of meat."

"Well, this marriage was your idea and from the way you parade around, I'm pretty sure you like me staring at your meat."

His eyes raked over her as she sat there in his shirt. They'd come back into the kitchen and eaten their cold dinner. Not that she was complaining. He'd come home with some pertinent information regarding her mother. At least they had a starting point, and she desperately clung to the hope that Lucas had provided.

"How can we get proof?" she asked, circling back to the main reason she'd gone to him in the first place. "I can't just ask the man if he's my father. I doubt he would even know how many love children he has running around."

Lucas slammed a plate into the dishwasher a little harder than she thought necessary. "Sterling has always been a bastard. Wouldn't surprise me a bit if he had more kids he ditched or women he lied to."

Why was he so irritated? Did it matter to Lucas if Sterling Perry was her father or not? Had Sterling done something to Lucas as well? Lucas was powerful in his own way, but Sterling was smarmy and vindictive.

"It's not like we can just go to the prison and ask," she muttered, thinking out loud.

"You're not going near that prison or that jerk," Lucas demanded. He started the dishwasher, then leaned against the counter and crossed his arms. "He's exactly where he belongs and I'll find the proof you need. That's why you came to me."

The conviction in his tone left no room for doubt. She knew Lucas was the best at his job and she knew he'd stop at nothing to find the truth for her. He was that kind of guy. His reputation didn't surprise her.

The man was known for seeking justice and putting his clients' needs at the top of his list. She had to assume he'd do the same for his wife.

But still, Paisley wished there was something she could do. She could always call Melinda. She was not only a friend, she also happened to be one of Sterling's daughters. Perhaps Paisley could casually ask if Melinda remembered Lynette. If Paisley could put her mom and Sterling together around the time of the pregnancy, then that would help in getting the proof they needed.

At some point, she'd have to go to Sterling, but she wasn't about to tell Lucas that. He wouldn't like her take-charge attitude, but she also didn't plan on sitting back and playing the dutiful little wife like he expected.

If she called Melinda and probed...

No. She couldn't do that. The woman's father was in jail. How insensitive would that be to start asking a bunch of questions?

But Paisley could call and offer her sympathies for all their family was going through. That conversation could always lead somewhere promising, right?

"Your silence worries me." Lucas closed the distance between them and stood before her. He tipped her chin up, so she stared at his chest then dragged her gaze to his eyes. "I remember you getting crazy ideas and they came right after you looked like you were staring off into space."

Paisley smiled. "I don't know what you're talking about."

"Leave this to me," he commanded. "You weren't able to figure this out on your own before and I know what I'm doing."

"You're suggesting I don't?" She rose to her feet and pushed his hand aside. "I don't need to be kept in the dark, and you said you'd work with me on this. That doesn't mean shoving me to the side so you can feed me only information you think I need to know."

His lips twitched. "You're sexy when you're angry."

Yeah, well, he was sexy all the time, but there was no sense in feeding his ego any more than necessary.

"Don't sidetrack me with sex." As if he hadn't been doing just that for the past three days. "I'm serious. I need to know the truth. Between the unknown father, my business and losing my mom…"

Emotions clogged her throat. Breaking down now would not help her get anywhere and the last person she wanted to look weak in front of was Lucas.

He immediately wrapped his arms around her and ran his hands up and down her back. "Your mom wouldn't want you to get so worked up," he assured her. "I'm not just going to leave you to deal with everything on your own."

He eased her back, swiping his thumbs across her damp cheeks. "Despite what you think, I married you for more than sex."

When he didn't elaborate, she worried.

He wanted a child—a topic they'd not discussed any more. But she wondered if there was more. Surely he didn't believe she'd just agree to something so…permanent.

There was definitely something else up with Lucas and until she knew what, she desperately needed to keep her heart guarded. Unfortunately, that was easier said than done because being with him again reminded her of how perfect they'd been in the past.

As if Paisley didn't have enough issues, what with a felon potentially being her father, being blackmailed into a marriage she was actually enjoying, losing her mother, losing all of her savings and her shop hanging on by a thread, now the horrid woman who stiffed her out of the expensive wedding dress was not replying to her messages.

This gave a whole new meaning to *runaway bride*.

Paisley gripped her steering wheel and

turned in to the new, partially renovated Texas Cattleman's Club location. She'd called Melinda yesterday after her talk with Lucas. Melinda had been so glad to hear from her, Paisley almost felt guilty about offering to take her mentor to lunch. But these were dire times and she wasn't going to stop pressing until she had the truth…no matter what that turned out to be.

Meeting at the clubhouse was a little bit intentional on Paisley's part. She knew Sterling's construction company was in charge of the renovations and, despite being in prison, he was vying for the top spot of president of TCC. Of course he had competition from Ryder Currin, the man who'd brought the club to Houston to begin with.

The whole ordeal was a mess, but being in the new café was a way to keep some focus on Sterling and have Melinda in the mind-set to discuss her father. Thankfully, Melinda was a TCC member or Paisley wouldn't be allowed in, seeing as how she wasn't a member.

As soon as Paisley stepped into the café, she scanned the rustic yet classy space. Here old-world charm met the Wild West. This café was definitely going to be a hot spot.

Paisley smiled as she found Melinda seated in the back. A little jumble of nerves formed in Paisley's belly. She didn't want to be completely self-centered with this meeting. She truly did love Melinda and wanted to catch up.

Her old mentor came to her feet and pulled Paisley into a hug.

"I was so happy you called," Melinda stated. "It's been too long."

Paisley eased back and reached for her chair. "It has. You know how it goes, though. Time just goes too fast. I've been so busy with the shop."

Melinda sat back down and offered a beaming smile. "How is your shop doing? Every time I drive by I daydream about those stunning dresses in your window. I choose a favorite and then you switch them out and I have a new favorite."

"Why do you think I swap them out so often? I can't decide which one I love more. But it's been difficult lately," Paisley said honestly. "I lost quite a bit of money and my savings, not to mention my mother lost everything she had when Sterling's... Well, you know the story."

Melinda winced and her smile vanished. "Oh, no, Paisley. I'm so, so sorry." Her friend shook her head and sighed. "I'm embarrassed, actually."

The waitress interrupted to get their drink orders, so they went ahead and ordered their food as well.

"You have nothing to be embarrassed for," Paisley said once they were alone again. "I can't imagine what you're going through having your father in jail. I'm the one who's sorry for you."

Melinda nodded and took in a deep breath. "It's been rough, but we'll get through."

Paisley knew her friend was made of tougher stuff than most. There was no doubt Melinda would be just fine, but Paisley had to probe…just a little. Melinda didn't dabble in the family business—she was so much more. She was a philanthropist and headed multiple charities. Those she worked on for struggling ranchers really put her in good graces with the Texas Cattleman's Club.

But Melinda was close with her father and maybe she knew more than she'd ever want to admit. But Paisley was desperate. If Sterling turned out to be her father, this marriage to Lucas could come to an end… before she got any more attached to her husband.

"Our situations aren't the same, but I understand the void," Paisley told her friend. "Since losing my mom, I've had a hard time figuring out my new normal. There are days I think I'm okay, but then something small and unexpected will remind me of what I lost."

Melinda reached across the table and gave Paisley's hand a reassuring squeeze. "I cannot even imagine. I never met your mother, but she had to have been remarkable."

"She was," Paisley said with a smile. "Lynette Morgan was one tough woman. She will be missed by so many."

Paisley purposely dropped her mother's name, hoping for a spark of recognition in Melinda's eyes.

Nothing. There was absolutely no flash of anything other than sympathy and sadness. Damn it.

"Let's discuss something else," Paisley suggested. "I didn't call you to hash out all of the bad that's happened."

Melinda nodded and pulled her hand back. "First, I do want you to know that I'm terribly sorry about what my father did and how it affected you. Well, you and the entire city of Houston. That was another reason I was glad you called. I really didn't know you were harmed by his actions, but

I don't have many friends lately, considering my last name. I think he's innocent, but he's still in jail, so maybe clearing his name is proving to be too difficult."

Paisley hated all of this for her friend. Melinda was nothing like Sterling Perry. Melinda was amazing, kind, generous. Sterling was… Well, Paisley wasn't wasting her mental space on him right now. She wanted to enjoy this lunch, even if she didn't get the answers she was hoping for.

Paisley reached for her water glass, and Melinda gasped.

"What is that rock?"

The woman immediately grabbed Paisley's finger and examined the rings from all angles, then shifted her focus back to Paisley.

"Congratulations." Melinda beamed. "Who's the lucky guy?"

Paisley swallowed. The rings on her finger still seemed so foreign and quite a bit over-the-top. Despite owning a bridal boutique, Paisley typically leaned toward the conservative side.

These rings Lucas had presented her with were anything but.

"Lucas Ford," Paisley stated. "We dated a long time ago and recently…reconnected."

Reconnected? Paisley inwardly groaned. She made it sound like they'd bumped buggies at the grocery and struck up a conversation about old times, when in fact, she'd turned to him for help and he'd blackmailed her and now she couldn't keep her clothes on around him.

But best to stick to the basics here, considering the real story was a mess and one that made her sound like a helpless female.

"I'm so happy for you," Melinda announced. "I hadn't heard about a wedding. Did you do something small?"

Of course a bridal shop owner would likely make the gossip fodder, but not this wedding. There was no press, no invitations or bridal showers. Paisley had been robbed of all of that, but every step of this was of her own making. She'd had to decide between her dream wedding to a man she loved or a quick ceremony with a man she could never love again.

"Actually, we flew to Vegas." There was no way to un-tacky their nuptials. "We didn't want to wait and since we're both nearly alone in the family department, we just didn't see a need for something large."

Thankfully the waitress brought their drinks and food and cut off any more wedding talk. The last thing Paisley wanted was to be asked about the gown or have to try to romanticize the day. She could just imagine Melinda's face were she to know about the tawdry lace jumpsuit.

"I'm just thrilled you found happiness," her friend said. "Hey, I'm having a cocktail party next week. I'd love for you to come."

A party sounded fun and she should try to incorporate more good times in her life considering she'd been in a whirlwind nightmare.

"I'd love that," Paisley stated. "Should I bring Lucas or leave him home?"

"Oh, bring him if you like. I'd love to see the newlyweds together."

"We'll be there," Paisley declared.

She made sure to keep the conversation steered toward Melinda because not only did Paisley not want to talk about the wedding, she also didn't want to talk about the husband. There may be no hiding the fact that she was indeed falling for him all over again.

# Eight

It was about damn time.

Sterling stepped into his country estate and breathed in the familiar scent of his home. Much better than that hellhole he'd been locked in.

Granted he was under house arrest, even after he'd paid millions to be released on bond. But he'd take house arrest over a cell any day. At least from home he had more power; he could control the strings of people around him and the outcome of his future.

First of all, he needed to get back in the saddle, so to speak, and make sure he was named president of TCC's Houston location. There was no way he'd lose to Ryder Currin. The man had had an affair with Sterling's wife, Tamara, years ago and Sterling was damn near positive Roarke was their love child. Sterling always claimed Roarke as his son, but never believed he truly was.

Roarke never agreed with how his father did business and Sterling wouldn't be a bit surprised if Roarke was the one feeding the lies to the media and the police about the whole financial debacle people were pinning on Sterling. Not to mention the damn murder.

He sure as hell never killed anyone.

Sterling just needed to get some rumors going about Roarke being Ryder's son. Sterling needed the upper hand to sabotage Ryder's bid for TCC President. There was only one person who could spread lies and gossip like wildfire and kerosene to help discredit Roarke.

Lavinia Cardwell.

Which was why his first order of business had been to invite his long-standing family friend over for a visit. Nothing like a catch-up session to kill two birds with one stone.

The first thing Sterling did while waiting on his guest to arrive was take a real shower with his thick towels and oversized walk-in shower with a rain head. There wasn't enough soap to wash off the grime from these past few weeks.

He'd just dressed and felt halfway normal when the doorbell chimed through the house. He'd made sure his staff was gone for the day, but he'd told his gate guard to let Lavinia up.

Sterling bound down the stairs, rehearsing exactly what he wanted to feed to the gossipmonger.

The moment he opened the door, Lavinia

threw her arms around him in a friendly hug and squeezed tight before easing back.

"It's so good to see you here," she said on a sigh of relief. "It's about time you got out."

Sterling couldn't agree more.

"It's good to see a friendly face," he replied, gesturing her inside. "Let's have a seat in the living room. Care for a drink?"

Lavinia stepped into the front room and shook her head. "No, thank you. But you have all you want. You've earned it."

He went to the bar in the corner and poured a shot of whiskey. "I sure as hell have. An innocent man shouldn't spend one second behind bars, let alone weeks."

Lavinia crossed her long legs and rested her arm on the sofa cushion. "I cannot even imagine how difficult that was. But I have to ask, do you know who set you up?"

*Here we go. Time to plant the seeds.*

"Do you think it was Angela?" she asked. "You two had been publicly fighting."

Sterling tipped back the shot and welcomed the burn. He set the glass on the bar and weighed his words carefully. Anything he said during their visit would be taken out into the public.

"No, I don't." He made his way to the sofa across from her and took a seat. "Angela and I may have quarreled over Ryder and her seeing each other, but she wouldn't do that to me. I wouldn't put it past Roarke, though."

Lavinia's brows rose. "Your son? I never would've thought of that."

Which was precisely why he was bringing it up now.

"Can I tell you something?" he asked, leaning forward for more of a dramatic effect.

"Of course. I'm here for you, Sterling."

"I think Roarke is Ryder's son." He let the words settle between them before he went on. "Tamara had an affair with Ryder Currin when he was just a stable hand. The timing fits for Roarke to be their love child, but I never said anything."

Lavinia gasped, her hand to her mouth. "You think Roarke set you up because he wanted you out of the way for his dad to be the club president?"

Sterling leaned back against the leather cushion and nodded. "I can't confirm this, but why else would he not stand by me when I needed my children the most? All of my kids have rallied around me, even Angela, and we've had our differences lately. Still, she believes in my innocence."

Lavinia pursed her lips. "This is all just so much to take in, but I see your point. I believe you were framed, but proving by whom will be difficult."

"I won't rest until the person behind all of this is found and punished," he vowed. "No matter who that turns out to be."

Even if that turned out to be the man he'd always considered a son.

# Nine

Lucas attempted to go through the boxes Paisley had given him from her mother's house, but all he found were old, useless receipts, some baby pictures of Paisley and a few past due notices on bills that were dated a few weeks before her death.

Nothing. The search so far had turned up absolutely nothing.

Everything Lucas had attempted had resulted in a dead end. But he wasn't done exploring avenues. He still had a few calls out, one being to the hospital where Paisley had been born. It was another long shot, but perhaps there was a nurse who remembered...hell, he didn't know. A wealthy man visiting a barmaid? Not the best description, but Lynette's photo might help.

Every aspect had to be touched on, no matter if it already seemed like a dead end. Exploring every part of people's pasts was what distinguished Lucas from other investigators.

Lucas prided himself on seeking justice and the truth. When he was a teen and Sterling Perry had taken advantage of his father, Lucas had vowed never to allow himself to be that vulnerable, that open to letting someone dupe him. He also knew one day he'd get revenge on Sterling... especially now that Lucas's late father wasn't around to do so himself.

And the timing of his plan revolved around Paisley. If she turned out to be Sterling's daughter, that would roll perfectly into getting close to the man and destroying him…all while not getting emotionally involved with his wife.

Lucas checked the time on his phone, noting there was no message from Paisley. She'd gotten up early and had gone to the boutique, but her shop had closed three hours ago. He absolutely hated that he cared, that he wanted to know where she was.

He hated even more that he let it bother him that she didn't consider this a real relationship. If she did, she'd be considerate enough to let him know where she was.

Damn it. Lucas stalked to his bar nestled in the corner of his penthouse. The wall of one-way windows gave him a picturesque view of their charming city, but right now, he didn't care. He was too pissed at himself for sliding into the role of doting husband a little too easily. He shouldn't care where she was; they had no real ties or expectations other than sex and him digging into Sterling. That was all they'd agreed upon.

Yet here he was brooding like a loser.

Sex could seriously cloud the vision. But even great sex with Paisley couldn't prevent him from destroying Sterling.

For completely selfish reasons, Lucas wanted him to be Paisley's father. That connection would certainly make the revenge that much sweeter since Sterling wasn't a fan of Lucas, either.

But for reasons he didn't want to delve into, Lucas almost hoped Sterling wasn't Paisley's father. She deserved so much better than an arrogant asshole whose every move was methodically thought out to what would benefit him most.

Lucas slammed back the bourbon and clanked his glass onto the mahogany bar top. He really should sip and enjoy the bourbon, but he was too on edge. His description of his potential father-in-law's actions could be applied to his own greed lately.

Wasn't that how he landed a pewter band on his finger?

Selfishness and greed. He'd never been

lumped with those terms before, but he was sure as hell owning them now.

The elevator chimed, indicating a key card had been used to access it.

Lucas poured another two fingers and curled his hand around the stemless glass. No way did he want to appear like he'd been waiting. She was free to come and go as she wanted, right?

Hell, he didn't know the rules to this type of marriage. He'd given her one—that she would be in his bed like a real wife and she'd more than obliged.

He was still holding his tumbler when the elevator door slid open and Paisley appeared. The topknot she'd left with this morning had come down and her hair tumbled around her shoulders.

She looked sexy as hell in that short, button-up navy dress with matching belt and a pair of nude heels that made her legs appear as if they went on for miles.

Lucas clenched his teeth as she set her stuff down on the table near the elevator.

She hadn't even looked his way, as if she didn't care if he was here or not.

Another niggle of irritation slid through him.

He was just about to say something— what, he wasn't sure—when Paisley rested her hands on the table where she'd dropped her purse. With her back to him, her head tipped down between her shoulders… shoulders that were shaking.

Ignoring the drink he'd poured, Lucas crossed the penthouse, his shoes clicking across the hardwoods. Just before he reached her, she jumped and spun around, her hand to her heart.

"I didn't see you here," she told him. "You startled me."

Clearly, she'd been in another world if she hadn't known he was in the same room. The smudged mascara beneath her eyes was like a punch to the gut. He never wanted to see tears on her, never wanted her to suffer for any reason. Despite their past and their messy present, that was one thing he couldn't handle.

"What happened?" he asked, swiping her damp cheeks. "Are you hurt?"

She shook her head. "No, just angry."

Angry tears. That was something he could work with, though he wished he didn't have to deal with tears at all.

"What happened?" he asked, ushering her into the living area.

"Just this bride who stiffed me for a bill that I can't possibly cover." She raked her hands down her face and sniffed. "It's ridiculous, really. I should've demanded payment in full before ordering such an extravagant gown, but she put down 20 percent and we had a contract for the rest. But the wedding got called off and she says the dress is just too painful to think about. She's refusing to pay the remainder."

Lucas listened as he eased her to the sofa beside him. He took one of her hands in his and squeezed it for silent reassurance.

"That was all via email, mind you," she

went on. "Each call I've tried to make has gone unanswered, my messages ignored. I spent this evening after I closed calling the bridesmaids that came in with her and ordered their dresses, but none of them was any help...other than the fact they had actually paid in full for theirs. Apparently the groom chose one of the bridesmaids, so they're all arguing."

And here he'd been getting irritated because she wasn't home when all she'd been doing was trying to save her business. He certainly couldn't fault her for that and he'd be a complete ass if he tried. Just because this marriage was based on revenge and blackmail didn't mean he was heartless. Lucas cared for her once, and he cared for her now, but in a completely different way.

Now he had his eyes open and his heart shut. He was well aware of what this was and what it wasn't.

Still, he'd vowed to help her with her business and he wasn't going to sit by and just let her be taken advantage of.

"Give me all of the information you have," he told her.

Paisley jerked her focus to him, her brows drawn in. "Why?"

"Because I track people down for a living. What do you mean why?"

"This isn't your battle to fight," she explained, pulling her hand from his. "I'm not asking for your help. I just told you all of that because you asked why I was crying. I tend to cry when I'm mad."

"I remember," he murmured, recalling a moment someone had stolen her purse when they'd gone to the movie theater. She'd burst into tears because her favorite lip gloss had been inside. "But I'm offering to help because that's what I told you I would do. I'm not going to let your business take this financial hit. When that woman ordered the dress, I'm sure you had her sign a contract, so she's liable. If you want, you could sue her. Just the threat might scare her into paying."

Paisley swiped beneath her eyes and

came to her feet. "The financial hit you're helping me with is the blow I took from the Ponzi scheme, not only from jilted brides."

She paced to the wall of windows and crossed her arms as she glanced out onto the city. Lucas remained on the sofa, watching her from across the room. Something churned in his gut, something he didn't want to put a finger on, didn't want to recognize.

The emotions he'd had for Paisley in the past hadn't completely died. A bond that strong couldn't, no matter how abrupt and shocking the ending had been.

That didn't mean he'd let himself get wrapped all around her again. Paisley didn't deserve some of the things that had happened to her, though. He wasn't about to just sit back and watch her livelihood destruct. That was one thing they still had in common—their drive to be the best at their careers.

She'd always wanted a bridal boutique. She'd always fantasized about their wedding when they'd been dating. He used to buy her hordes of bridal magazines back in the day and she would pore over them for hours.

"I just want her to pay," she finally stated, turning back to face him. "I'll give you her name and the contract she signed when she ordered the dress. Threaten legal action if necessary. I just want my thirty-five thousand dollars."

Lucas jerked. "For a dress? What the hell is it made of? Gold blocks?"

Paisley smoothed her hair over one shoulder and rolled her eyes. "Actually, it was hand sewn and the beading is from Italy. The designer is quite popular among celebrities and only a select clientele can even think about purchasing a Bella gown."

"Is that why you went with scraps of lace?"

Paisley's eyes narrowed. "Don't think it didn't cross my mind to stick you with a giant bill for a Bella gown. She's my favorite designer, but I opted to be spiteful in another way."

Lucas came to his feet and slowly crossed to her. Those eyes remained locked on him and the way she looked at him, like she used to seconds before she ripped his clothes off, had his body already stirring to life.

"By driving me out of my mind?" he asked as he closed in on her.

"Exactly." She tipped her chin and smiled. "Don't act like you didn't love seeing me. I know you, Lucas. Things might be different now, but you're still a man with basic wants and desires."

He snaked an arm around her waist and pulled her body to his. "There's nothing basic about my wants and desires for you, Tart. Never has been. You know exactly what buttons to push to make me ache for you even when you're not here."

Her brow quirked as her gaze darted to his lips.

"I missed you tonight." Damn it. He hadn't meant to let that slip.

"You mean I didn't check in?" she asked. "Are we back to those archaic rules of yours?"

"That's not what I meant." When she gave him another eye roll, he corrected himself. "Okay, fine. Maybe that's what I meant, but is it wrong that I want to know what's going on with my wife?"

She shuddered in his arms, and he wasn't sure if it was from anger over his words or if she was turned on.

"Is that the type of marriage we have?" she asked, still staring at him, her eyes searching for answers. "We check in with each other and discuss dinner or grocery lists and schedules? Because that's not the impression I had."

Lucas clenched his jaw and reached up to toy with the ends of her hair. He stared at the strands between his fingertips and weighed his next words. Every time she brought up their marriage she made him sound like a lovesick husband from the '50s. And damn it, she was right.

Not the lovesick part. But they did need some sort of boundaries before moving forward.

"Maybe we need to discuss what each of us expects," he stated, pushing her hair back over her shoulder and trailing his hand down the column of her neck. "Besides me saving your business and finding out about Sterling."

"Oh, so the baby is off the list now?"

Her mocking tone had him biting the inside of his cheek as he stared into her gaze. "No, actually it's not. But I thought we could keep this a little more…"

"Simple?"

Lucas nodded and circled her waist with both hands. He couldn't be this close and not touch her. He wanted to unfasten each of those little buttons and expose whatever sexy lingerie she wore beneath the dress, because he knew Paisley. She loved lace and satin.

"How about if I make dinner three nights a week and have it ready when you get home?" he suggested.

Paisley's brows rose. "Are you joking?"

"I don't want to make your life with me miserable."

She shook her head. "I'm just surprised you offered to cook. What about the other four nights?"

Lucas shrugged. "We'll order out or I'll take you wherever you want."

Her gaze narrowed and she pursed her lips. "Do you think all of this is going to make me give in to being your baby mama?"

Lucas couldn't help but laugh at her. "No, I didn't think things would be that simple."

Hell, he sounded ridiculous now, but seeing her so upset, well…damn it. He'd wanted to help. Was that absurd for her to believe?

"I don't have to be the enemy here," he defended.

Paisley stared at him for a moment before surprising him by wrapping her arms around him and burying her face in his neck.

"I don't know what you are, but right now I need you," she murmured before easing back slightly. "I don't have many people I can count on and I don't know what your angle is quite yet, but I have to trust you. For now, anyway."

He didn't like that niggle of guilt. He sure as hell didn't like that she doubted him and how much she could trust him. His revenge wasn't on her, but Sterling. Yes, he was using her to get to the old bastard, but he didn't want her hurt.

Lucas couldn't help but worry that no matter the outcome, a part of Paisley would be crushed. She wanted to have a father, especially since her mother was gone, but did she truly want one who was so deceptive and slimy?

"What do you say you get me that information on the bride and I'll call for takeout?" Lucas suggested.

Paisley tipped her head. "I can't believe you're not trying to get me out of my clothes."

Lucas laughed and started working on that top button. "I never said anything to the contrary. In fact, I say we have a naked picnic."

"At some point I really need to resist you," she grumbled.

Lucas moved down to the next button. "But not now."

"No." She took a deep breath, her breasts straining against the next button. "Not now."

He finished the trail of buttons and parted the material. When Lucas took a step back, he thought about forgoing dinner and the bride and just getting to his wife.

She stood before him in a nude lace bra and panty set and those heels, and she wasn't even trying to be sexy, she simply was. The woman was absolutely breathtaking after a bad day and a crying jag.

Would he ever get to the point he didn't want her?

"If you keep looking at me like that, we won't get dinner." She sauntered around him and headed toward the hallway. "And I do believe it's your night to cook."

Yeah. She was definitely going to be the death of him.

But what a way to go.

# Ten

Paisley just finished a consultation with a bride renewing her vows when her cell rang. She glanced at the screen, surprised to see Lucas's name. He typically only texted or he would just pop in.

She swiped the screen and answered.

"Sterling is out on bail," Lucas declared.

The bomb he dropped had her knees weakening, her heart beating fast, her head spinning.

Paisley eased down into her desk chair and pulled in a deep breath. "When did he get out?"

"Apparently last night on several millions in bail," Lucas stated. "I wanted to tell you as soon as I found out."

She glanced to the antique clock on her desk, more for decoration than functionality. She calculated how much time she had left until her boutique closed, and how soon she could make it to Sterling's estate when she left.

"Don't even think about it," Lucas warned.

"You don't know what I'm thinking," she countered, gripping her phone tighter.

"Tart, I know you and you're trying to figure out how to go talk to him without me knowing."

She didn't care if Lucas knew or not. Right now all she thought about was time and how soon she could talk to the man who may very well be her father.

"Well, why wouldn't I want to go there?" she exclaimed. "He obviously knew my mother. Maybe she told him the truth all those years ago. He's the only one who could have all the answers."

Lucas exhaled loudly and Paisley could practically see him rubbing his head trying to maintain his patience. She'd hired him to find the truth, though she wasn't exactly paying.

Regardless, there was no reason she couldn't continue working her angles. Maybe Sterling didn't know anything, but she had to ask. Seeing him face-to-face would be the only way to tell if he was lying about his knowledge of her mother. This was too important to do over the phone and she didn't want to wait.

"Let me handle this," he finally told her. "I'm not trying to keep you out, but I do have a method and a plan. I promise, when the time comes to confront him, I will drive you there myself."

Paisley wanted to argue, she wanted to hang up, close her shop and head straight to Sterling Perry's house. But the other part of her knew Lucas was right. He did this for a living, plus she'd gone to him for his help, so going against it would only be counterproductive. She fully believed he had her best interests at heart. If he wanted to keep things from her, he never would've told her about Sterling's release.

Paisley just wished the process would speed up so she could know once and for all.

"I won't go," she conceded. "But I don't like this."

"Duly noted," he replied with a low chuckle. "I'm going to be late tonight, but I'm having your favorite Thai food delivered at seven. I figured that would give you enough time to get home, unwind, have a glass of wine or whatever."

Well, damn. Hard to be upset with the man when he was sticking to his plan of being in charge of dinner each night. Why did he have to do these little things that made her fall more and more for him?

"That wasn't necessary," she told him. "But I'm not about to turn down my favorite dinner."

"I didn't figure you would," he chuckled. "There's also a little surprise waiting at home for you."

*At home.*

The two words seemed to symbolize so much—like the possibility that they were creating a real life together and not some temporary arrangement that stemmed from blackmail.

"I love surprises," she told him. "But you don't have to do that."

"I know I don't," he stated. "Don't get your hopes up, though. The surprise is nothing major."

Maybe not to him, but the fact he'd thought of her enough to even have a surprise said so much. Paisley's heart swelled at the idea that he wanted to give her something for no reason. But she couldn't let her mind travel to the place her heart already resided. Some part of her had to remain logical and firmly planted in reality. All of this was temporary. No matter how much she was falling for him, no matter how much she wished they could start something real, he only wanted her for a child and she needed him to find out the truth.

They weren't the same people they once were, so the love and trust they'd need to start a solid foundation just wasn't there yet.

Yet. As if he was going to fall madly in love with her and want a real future together.

"I need to run," he told her, interrupting her thoughts. "I might be late, so you don't need to wait up."

He disconnected the call, and Paisley set her cell down as she leaned back in her seat, processing the whole Sterling update. What would he say when she confronted him? Would he deny her or welcome her into the fold of the family?

Granted, that was if she ended up being his daughter. Paisley wanted so desperately to feel like she belonged somewhere. Oh, she'd never admit as much, because she was trying to be the independent woman she claimed. But right now, she was getting hit from all sides and, well, she was a bit needy. There was no room for pride when everything had been taken away.

Everyone had a vulnerable point in their life and she had to admit, she'd reached hers.

She wasn't going to stay down long, though. She would climb back up out of this nightmare of losing her mother, not knowing her father, marrying a man who didn't love her and nearly losing her business. She'd ultimately find love and have a family like she always dreamed. Unfortunately, she just had to take the long way to get there.

With renewed hope that something in her favor would happen soon, Paisley went to work at her computer for the vow renewal bride. There was much to be done to keep other people's dreams fulfilled until she could get to her own.

* * *

With every corner he turned leading to another dead end, Lucas opted to head to the new TCC clubhouse. He'd been there for the grand party in the ballroom several weeks ago, but hadn't been since.

The renovations were nearly complete in the old historical Houston building, though there were definitely areas that weren't done. The ballroom, the café, several of the upstairs units, those were all finished. The outdoor area and several of the offices still had a way to go. But they shouldn't take too much longer.

Then the race would be on to see who the new president was. The Perry/Currin feud would never end at this rate. The decades-old rivalry kept carrying over from generation to generation, and there always seemed to be some new drama to bicker about.

They made the Capulets and the Montagues look like preschool playmates.

Lucas almost wished Paisley wasn't related to anyone in that mess.

He figured coming to the clubhouse now that Sterling was out might give him some insight. Or at the very least, there would be gossip. Everything he could gather on Sterling could potentially be used. From what Lucas had heard, the man's own son hadn't bothered to help. Roarke was a crusading attorney and hadn't once offered assistance to Sterling.

That said quite a bit about Sterling's character. Though, in Roarke's defense, he hadn't been all that close to his father. The two clashed more often than not and had been known to have public arguments. But still, wouldn't a son come to the aid of his father in a situation this dire?

Just before Lucas had come to the clubhouse, he'd gotten a call from the hospital where Paisley was born. There was a night nurse who was still on the same unit, but she couldn't answer any questions. Privacy laws were the main reason, but she also just didn't remember.

He had to at least try, though he'd figured that angle would be another dead end.

There had to be some trace to Paisley's biological father, but Lucas had yet to find it. She deserved to know if that letter from her mother meant anything or if Lynette had just been guessing herself.

Maybe they could be bold enough to show Sterling the letter and demand a DNA test. Lucas wasn't sure Sterling would be so quick to cooperate, considering he had a mess in his life already without adding a long-lost child.

Not that Lucas would say this to Paisley, but her mother had been notably seen with many men over the years. She'd dated quite a bit. Being a barmaid back in the day, well, perhaps she'd taken more than one wealthy man home for the night.

Lucas sure as hell wasn't judging what anyone did in their free time. He was just trying to zero in on who Lynette associated herself with back then. Lucas already had another meeting set up with the bar owner. He figured going back in when the place wasn't slammed and noisy would be a better option, plus he'd wanted to give the guy some time to jog his memory. Now that Lucas had already questioned him, there was no doubt the old guy was thinking back.

The mind was just wired that way. Once the past was mentioned, people tended to dwell on it over the next several days, sometimes weeks, and other memories would come to them.

Lucas was banking on that happening. He wasn't letting up on this at all...no matter what the outcome.

He stepped up to the bar and ordered a beer on tap. A local brewery had worked a deal with the TCC clubhouse. Lucas was all for supporting local businesses...except for Sterling. Lucas hoped like hell that man didn't become the new president. Sterling was the last person who should be given more authority.

Lucas was already making mental notes about grabbing more boxes from Paisley's stash of her mother's things when a hand clamped down on his shoulder.

He glanced around to see Ethan Barringer, the CEO of Perry Construction. Sterling owned a multitude of companies through Perry Holdings, but Ethan was one of his main men.

"Haven't seen you around here," Ethan commented as he settled on a stool next to Lucas. "Been keeping busy?"

Lucas nodded and accepted the frosty mug from the bartender. "Just now getting a chance to come back and see the place. It's really coming together."

Ethan nodded and curled his hands around his own beer. "This old building had some stumbling blocks, but we're definitely seeing the light at the end of the tunnel."

"Heard Sterling was out."

Ethan took a long pull of his drink, but Lucas kept his eyes on the guy. He liked Ethan well enough. It wasn't his fault his employer was a bastard.

"Yeah. House arrest," Ethan added. "He's determined to find out who set him up. I just heard a rumor that Roarke might actually be Ryder's son and not Sterling's. Sterling's just in a hell of a mess right now and I'm not sure when things will clear for him."

Lucas was glad he'd swallowed his drink before that little bombshell was dropped. What the hell kind of twists and turns did Sterling have in his life? His own son wasn't actually his son? And he may have an illegitimate daughter?

The man was a walking soap opera.

Lucas could hardly keep up with the chaos that seemed to always surround Sterling. Was this really a guy anyone would consider for president of the most elite club in Texas?

"That would certainly put a spin on

things if that turned out to be true," Lucas muttered, taking another sip of his beer.

"Who knows what's going to happen," Ethan commented with a shake of his head. "I feel like the past few weeks have been all ups and downs and one surprise after another. For all of us, really."

Lucas shifted in his seat and nodded in agreement. Houston certainly had its share of drama lately and it seemed no one was left out.

"Is that a wedding band?" Ethan asked, gesturing toward Lucas's hand.

"Yeah. A little over a week ago, actually. I married Paisley Morgan."

A wide smile spread across Ethan's face. "Congrats, man. Let me buy your beer. Marriage is a wonderful thing when you find the right person. I couldn't imagine life without Aria Jensen."

Ethan and Aria had been friends turned lovers and they both played a huge roll in the Houston Club.

While he was thrilled for the happy couple, Lucas didn't really want to get into the whole marriage and love talk with Ethan... or with anyone, really. The arrangement he had with Paisley worked for them. They might not be in love, but they had a history, and they knew each other more than most married couples. They might be different people now, but they still had a bond that time and pain couldn't erase.

"You're a lucky man," Lucas stated, making sure to keep the topic on Ethan. "Not many people find their soul mate."

"I'd say we're both lucky," Ethan commented. "With all the chaos in this town, we need to cling to something good."

Lucas couldn't agree more. Only the "good" he was clinging to was the promise that he'd seek justice against Sterling for all the crooked dealings and people he'd betrayed.

Paisley was in that mix, so in a sense he was seeking justice for her, too. He kept reminding himself of that so he didn't focus on the guilt he felt from using her to get to Sterling.

Lucas finished his beer, more than ready to get home to his wife. This new rumor could prove to be extremely useful in their journey, but Lucas still wasn't ready to confront Sterling. He wanted a better timeline and a way to put him and Lynette together before Paisley was born. Maybe the affairs coincided. Revenge affairs weren't uncommon.

Lucas couldn't imagine being married to one woman and wanting another. Loyalty meant everything to him.

Suddenly, Lucas was more eager to get home. He'd never had someone waiting for him before and he knew this was something he shouldn't get accustomed to...but that didn't stop him from enjoying what he had now.

Paisley kept saying this marriage was temporary, but he knew her and knew that was her defense mechanism. She was afraid, but what she didn't realize was that he was, too. Having her back in his life, back in his bed, terrified him. Because if she walked away again, he wasn't sure if he could rebuild his heart a second time.

# Eleven

"What do you say we go away?"

Angela Perry slid her arms up around Ryder Currin's neck and threaded her fingers through his hair. She worried so much about the turmoil surrounding her family. But she and Ryder needed a chance to just be themselves without all the rest of the messy outside world getting in.

She was falling for him and she needed him to realize this was serious for her. Could they have a future together even though he was much older and his family and hers had been rivals for decades?

The rivalry didn't matter to her, though it mattered heavily to her father. Angela couldn't live her life to please her father.

Sterling had been released from prison last night and Angela feared they'd go back into a verbal sparring match over her relationship with Ryder. She'd yet to visit him. While she fully believed in her father's innocence, she wanted him to understand that he couldn't control who she wanted to spend her time with.

"Just the two of us," she went on, loving how Ryder wrapped his arms around her waist and pulled her close. "Maybe fly to the mountains and get a cozy cabin. Or, if you prefer me in a skimpy suit, we could go to the beach."

Ryder pulled in a deep breath, and she knew from that second of hesitation that he would make an excuse or give a justifiable reason why they shouldn't go. She didn't want to hear all the reasons why this might be a bad idea. All she cared about was why they should escape and put their relationship above all else. But she didn't want to argue in the few stolen moments they had together.

"It's okay," she quickly continued. "I know there's so much going on and it's—"

"Not that I don't want to," he interjected. "I'd love nothing more than to get away with you for a few days and forget we have a whole host of issues."

"Then let's do it," she urged. "What's a few days? I swear, every issue will be waiting for us when we return, so we might as well ignore them for a bit."

Ryder reached up and smoothed her hair from her face. The wind kicked up and wrapped them in the evening summer air. What she wouldn't give to be somewhere else with him right this moment instead of in Houston where her father was out on bail and no doubt ready to fight, where there was an unidentified dead body that her father was framed in the murder of, and where the whole financial scheme seemed to touch everyone she knew.

When her father caused a mess, he caused a hell of a disaster. She honestly didn't believe he had killed someone—he wasn't vicious. He might be egotistical and greedy, but he wasn't a killer. Still, he had that black cloud looming over him, and she couldn't help but worry the drama would trickle down onto her.

The feud between her father and her lover…

Angela closed her eyes and rested her head in the crook of Ryder's neck. She inhaled the familiar scent she only associated with him and attempted to calm herself.

Would they ever just get peace? Could they ever truly be happy or would something, or someone, constantly be trying to pry them apart?

"I'll take you anywhere you want to go."

Angela jerked back, unable to stop the smile. "Seriously?"

Ryder covered her lips with his before easing away just enough to reply, "Yes.

You deserve it. Hell, we deserve it. Pick the place and I'll have my jet ready."

Ryder Currin was a workaholic, but she also knew he'd do anything for her. She thought herself lucky that Ryder wanted to be with her, considering the feud, but that was just a testimony to how strong their bond was. Angela refused to let anyone come between them, including her powerful father. She and Ryder together were a dynamic couple and could forge through anything.

"Better yet," he amended, "I'll surprise you. Give me a few days to get things lined up and some work settled and I'll take you away."

Angela couldn't even explain the excitement that rushed through her. Finally, they were going to escape and just be a real couple with no problems. The idea of getting away with Ryder thrilled her and she couldn't wait to see where he decided to take her.

Her father had pointed out that Ryder

was too old for her, but Angela didn't care about age. She cared about how a man treated her, how he put her first, and Ryder did just that. He was romantic and loving and selfless...exactly what Angela needed in her messy life right now. Not to mention what she wanted in her future.

But, now that her father was home, she couldn't guarantee he wouldn't double down his efforts to cause trouble and tear them apart. Even if he was under house arrest, Sterling Perry's arms reached far and wide. When he wanted something, people reacted swiftly and effectively.

Angela nuzzled back into Ryder and already started a mental countdown to their romantic getaway. She refused to let anyone or anything stand in their way of happiness.

*The bastard was out on bail. How the hell could that have happened?*

*Oh, right. Money. Something I'd never*

*have enough of to simply pay off my sins and make people drop and obey my every command.*

*Sterling had to take the fall for murder. I wouldn't go down for something that I'd done only to protect myself.*

*Maybe Sterling hadn't done the actual crimes he was incarcerated for, but he'd sure as hell done plenty of others. He was a complete bastard and nearly everyone could agree to that.*

*I wouldn't get caught. I had a plan and nobody would get in my way. Not the police, not Sterling.*

*I was making my own way through life and it wouldn't be long before people took notice and respected me.*

Paisley had just slid her satin gown over her head when she heard the chime from the elevator. She glanced to the clock and wondered what Lucas's version of late actually was. He'd told her she didn't have to wait up, but it was only eight o'clock.

She stepped into the living area just as the elevator door slid open. Lucas's eyes immediately met hers and she got that giddy, aroused feeling she always did when she saw him. Maybe that young girl who'd been in love with him was still inside there. She was hopeful something could come from this crazy arrangement.

But the woman who was married to him? Well, she had to be a bit more realistic. She enjoyed the sex and the living arrangement, but she also knew it would come to an end.

"Thanks for my surprise." Paisley gestured toward the coffee table with a giant bowl full of Sweetarts—hence the name he'd dubbed her years ago. "The Thai food was amazing and so was the candy. I also managed a glass of wine and a good book. It's been a great night."

He unbuttoned his sleeves and rolled them up his forearms, then undid the top two buttons of his shirt as he stalked toward her.

"So you're saying you didn't need me?" he joked with a naughty grin.

"I need you for other things," she told him, purposely raking her gaze down his lean body. "I thought you were going to be late," she added.

Lucas pulled the black Stetson off his head and ruffled a hand through his hair, leaving it messy, sexy.

"I went to the clubhouse hoping there would be some buzz about Sterling's release," he said. "Ethan Barringer was there and I found out something that could affect our plans."

Paisley reached for his arm and stared into his eyes. "What happened?"

"First of all, you know Sterling is out, but he's under house arrest. Clearly, he's not going anywhere, but that won't stop his cronies from coming to him."

"Okay. What else?"

Lucas's mouth twitched and she couldn't

tell if he was amused or stunned. "There's a new rumor that Roarke isn't Sterling's son."

Paisley gasped. "What?"

"I don't know if it's true, but if it is, that would explain why Roarke wasn't at his father's side or working to free him."

"You think Roarke knows Sterling isn't his father?" she asked, her mind trying to process what all this could mean.

Lucas trailed a fingertip up her arm and curled his hand over her shoulder. "I don't know anything yet, but I wanted to keep you informed. We need to figure out our next steps. I really need to find some- thing that will put Sterling and your mom together before you were born. You and Roarke are about the same age, so maybe there's some backstory there that we're missing."

Paisley nodded in agreement, but she had no clue how to go about finding the truth about illicit affairs. Again, these were things only Sterling could reveal because everyone else—her mother and Sterling's wife—had passed on.

"Do you think Sterling cheated on his wife because she cheated on him first or vice versa?" she asked.

Good grief. Was nobody faithful? Were she and Roarke both love children spawned from lust and revenge?

"I think it's worth exploring," he told her as he slid his hand down her back and pulled her against him. "I planned on going back to the office and working more, but after I left the clubhouse, I just wanted to get home."

Paisley shouldn't let his charming words affect her so, but she couldn't help herself. Lucas was getting to her more and more each day. She wasn't even sure he was deliberately trying to use his charms to spin her farther into his web. He was just naturally appealing.

How could she not fall for the man he'd become? Successful, strong, protective…

he was the entire package. And their past bond only pulled her in deeper.

"Well, I'm glad you're here," she admitted. "I wasn't looking forward to going to bed without you."

Those blue eyes raked down her body as he reached for the straps on her gown. "It's a bit too early for bed, isn't it?"

Paisley shivered as the satin slid over the swell of her breasts and grazed her sensitive nipples. She pulled in a deep breath and relished the instant arousal and the hunger in his eyes.

"I'm not tired," she told him. "Did you have something in mind?"

Lucas's lips twitched. "I have in mind to rip this gown off you, but I'm also enjoying your slow striptease."

"It's not a striptease if you're the one doing the stripping," she informed him.

Before he could say a word, Paisley stepped back. Keeping her eyes locked on his, she slid her thumbs into the fabric at her waist and very carefully, methodically, eased the material down. The gradual way it slid over her body only awakened her senses even more. She couldn't wait for him to get his hands on her.

They'd been intimate every single day since they'd married and the need to be with him continued to grow. Being physical was easy. The hard part was all the emotions that were going to hold her hostage in this marriage.

Paisley stepped out of the gown and stood before Lucas completely bare. Once again, he raked that hungry gaze over her and she couldn't begin to say who was actually in charge here. She may have him spellbound by being naked, but all he had to do was give her that heavy-lidded look or a crook of his finger and she turned into a puddle of desire.

"Do you ever wear anything under your clothes?" He took a step toward her. "Not that I'm complaining."

"Are you implying I'm not ladylike?" she retorted. "I love my teddies beneath my dresses. They're comfortable and keep all my rolls smoothed out, which works out well because I love candy, as you well know."

Lucas laughed as his hands circled her waist. "Your rolls are sexy, the teddies are sexy, though I realize you use them for other reasons than to drive me crazy."

"You feed me dinner every night, surprise me with my favorite candy, call my extra pounds sexy... Better watch it, Lucas. I might not want to end this marriage, after all."

Something shifted in his eyes, something she couldn't quite pinpoint. Did he truly want to stay married to her? What if she did remain in this marriage? What if they had children like they'd once dreamed? She wanted to know his thoughts on her, on the marriage. Could he see a real future here?

Just because their lives had changed drastically, did that mean their original goals when they'd been young had to change as well? Perhaps that twentysomething couple had been smarter than she gave them credit for. They'd had it all figured out... until she'd walked away.

"Maybe we can come to an agreement that works for both of us," he countered.

Before she could reply, Lucas leaned down and slid his lips over hers. The slow, easy way he made love to her mouth only added to the ever-growing anticipation and arousal. They'd typically been so hot for each other, their clothes were removed in a frantic flurry.

But right now, with his delicate touch, the way he seemed to explore her kiss as if for the first time, Paisley wondered what had overcome him. It was almost like he was getting to know her all over again.

In a move she didn't expect, Lucas removed his lips from hers and swept her up into his arms. She smiled as she looped her arms around his neck and threaded her fingers through his hair.

She thought he would take a few steps to

the couch since they always just went with the closest surface, but he carried her down the hall toward their master suite.

The man was full of romance tonight and he was spoiling her for any type of a future without him.

Lucas set her down on her feet next to the side of the bed. With gentle hands, he forced her to lie down before he stepped back and started undressing. His gaze never wavered as he slowly exposed himself in all his magnificent, naked glory.

Lucas Ford was a stunning man. With his sculpted muscles in all the right places and that wicked grin, Paisley couldn't ignore the lust that slammed into her. But her attraction went beyond lust and she was well aware that love had entered back into the mix.

That was something she certainly would not be sharing with him. They had more pressing things to tend to than her emotions...which she doubted he reciprocated.

Lucas dropped to his knees before her and Paisley rose up on her elbows, eager to watch whatever he was about to do. He took one of her feet in hand and began massaging it. Not the body part she thought he was going for, but she certainly wasn't complaining.

His thumb slid over her arch and Paisley nearly groaned from the sensation. Nobody had ever given her a foot massage.

Oh, mercy, those hands were talented.

He thoroughly gave attention to one foot before releasing it and moving to the other. As she stared down at the top of his head, she couldn't believe this was the position she was in. Not literally this moment, but the marriage to Lucas, the fact that she wanted it to keep going and see if they could build on this shaky foundation.

Paisley's eyes nearly rolled back in her head when Lucas slid his hands up her calves and continued this amazing massage. Then he traveled up to the knee, where he placed a gentle kiss on the inside of each one.

He was driving her out of her ever loving mind and she wouldn't trade this for anything.

Lucas's eyes came up to meet hers as his hands grazed up to her thighs. There it was again—that naughty grin that had her squirming at his silent promise.

"You're going awfully slow tonight," she complained.

Those thumbs moved up again, closer to her core where she ached the most. He was enjoying this bout of torture.

"Have I ever left you hanging?" he asked, sliding one finger into her.

Paisley's hips bucked as she gripped handfuls of the duvet. A moan was her only reply. Did he actually expect her to talk?

"That's what I thought," he murmured before he replaced that finger with his mouth.

Paisley thought she heard him mutter something about needing her, but she was too lost to comprehend anything but his touch.

Lucas grabbed hold of her hips as he pleasured her in a way he'd never done before. Paisley went between glancing down to him to tossing her head back and shutting her eyes to lock in the moment.

Her body responded in no time and she spiraled completely out of control. Lucas never let up as he continued meeting her every need and making love to her in a way that took their intimacy to a different level.

Finally, her body settled, the tremors ceased and Paisley was positive she'd never move again.

But Lucas crept up her body, placing kisses on her abdomen and massaging her breasts.

"Sorry about that," he muttered between kisses. "I was trying to give you a body massage and got sidetracked."

Paisley dropped onto her back and flung an arm over her eyes. "I've never had a massage quite like that."

He eventually came all the way up and pressed her deeper into the mattress with his weight. His arms rested on either side of her head as he smiled down at her.

"I'll be the only one giving you massages," he told her. "This body is all for me."

Paisley thrust her fingers through his coarse hair and shifted her body to turn them over. Lucas went onto his back, and she straddled him. Her hair curtained them both as she looked down onto his surprised face.

"I think it's my turn to massage something," she warned. "Plus, I need to show you my thanks for the dinner, the candy and for working so hard on my case."

Lucas curled his fingers into her backside and urged her exactly where she wanted to be. The second she sank down onto him, every needy, achy emotion came rushing back.

"Do your thing, Tart." He smiled as he

moved her hips with his. "I do love to be rewarded."

Paisley proceeded to show him just how grateful she was…and she tried to tell herself that falling for him again was a huge mistake.

Unfortunately, it was too late.

# Twelve

"And if you want to remove the veil from the headpiece for the reception, that's always an option."

Paisley assisted the bride and showed her the transformation, which earned a gasp from the bride's mother and best friend who sat next to the stage and curved mirrors.

"You have to get it," the beaming friend said with a dramatic clap of her hands. "You look like royalty."

It was true. Paisley loved each of her

customers and reveled in watching their dream wedding unfold before her eyes. Part of Paisley should be bitter for having been robbed of her special day, but that was all on her. She could've said no. She could've figured out another way.

But part of her still wanted Lucas after all these years. She'd never wanted to end things with him in the first place. If his father hadn't intervened and caught a naive young Paisley off guard, there was no doubt in her mind they'd be married...for the right reasons.

Perhaps even by this time they would have little baby Fords running around, probably even in school.

Even though they'd been separated, she had to admit being married to him was working out much better than she ever would've thought. She never felt used or like she was a burden to him. In fact, she'd swear that he had feelings for her, but she just couldn't bring that up.

Not when the case was hovering over

them and he had made it quite clear he wanted her to have his child.

She'd first thought that idea was preposterous, but now…if she could clear out all the mess surrounding them and they could start with a solid foundation, Paisley would jump at the chance to start a family with Lucas.

"I want the veil and the dress," the bride gushed, pulling Paisley back into the moment. "They're so perfect for the venue and my style. Now, moving onto accessories and shoes."

Paisley smiled at the bride's reflection in the wall of mirrors. "I can pull some of my favorites and then we can go from there. What size shoe?"

"Eight."

While Paisley went to the accessory room, she heard the bell on the door chime. She poked her head out and was surprised to see her husband.

Her stomach did a flip and she hated that he looked way better than any man had a right to. It was just last night they'd made love and cuddled. That hadn't happened since they'd married. They'd only had fast, frantic sex and gone their separate ways. But last night was different. Last night had thrust her back to a time when nothing else had existed but the two of them. When she'd thought for sure she would spend her life with Lucas Ford.

As much as she wanted to believe that could be a possibility, she had to guard her heart until this ordeal was settled and she knew the truth about her father. She really didn't want to think of a future family when she didn't have her past family figured out.

As soon as Lucas spotted her, he crossed the space and kissed her cheek, then laid a quick, toe-curling kiss on her lips.

"What are you doing here?" she asked, trying to regain her mental balance.

"You're closing soon, so I thought I'd take you to dinner."

She glanced over her shoulder and spotted the party of three ladies all smiling and staring in her direction. No doubt they caught sight of the kisses.

"I might be a bit longer," she murmured. "I need to help this bride finalize her look."

Lucas shrugged and glanced around the shop. "No problem. I can just have a seat and wait. Don't rush."

Not that she wasn't thrilled he was taking her out, but having him hang around while she worked was a bit unnerving. Still, she knew it would be a vain attempt to get him to leave or wait somewhere else, so she didn't argue the point.

Paisley grabbed several earrings, bracelet and necklace options and took them back out to the bride.

"Is that your husband?" the mother of the bride asked.

Paisley nodded as she laid out the black velvet display board for everyone to see. She had her favorites, but she never said which until the bride made her opinion known.

"You are one lucky woman," the lady replied.

Paisley merely smiled. "Thank you."

"Newlyweds?" she guessed.

"We've been married two weeks."

The bride gasped. "Oh, congratulations! I already noticed your killer rings. They're stunning. I bet you had a gorgeous wedding, too."

Paisley resisted the urge to laugh, but merely nodded and smiled. "It was quite memorable."

After about thirty minutes of debating, Paisley finally got the bride all settled with her dress, veil, shoes and accessories. Once they were gone, Paisley turned the sign and flicked the lock on the door.

"You are remarkable."

She turned and tipped her head. "Excuse me?"

Lucas should look ridiculous all relaxed on the white chaise, but he looked...perfect. Damn it. The man always looked perfect. She likely looked haggard since he'd kept her up most of the night and she'd logged in a full ten hours at the shop.

"With your customer," he added. "She was clearly nervous and not taking advice from her mother and you somehow found a middle ground and made them both happy."

Paisley smoothed her hand down her red sheath dress and headed for the dressing room to start gathering up the gown rejects.

"That's what most of my job consists of, believe it or not. Moms always see their daughters as little girls playing dress up, so they have their own idea of what the gown should be. But the bride has been dreaming of this moment for her entire life and she has her own idea."

Paisley smoothed the heavy drapes aside and entered the oversize dressing area. There were only three gowns that needed to be put back. These were all the mother's top picks, unfortunately.

"Did you have dreams with your mother?" he asked, following her inside.

The slam of emotions hit her hard, and Paisley's hands stilled on the zipper. She drew in a deep breath and swallowed the lump in her throat.

"I've always had a dream about my wedding," she replied, going back to the task and not turning to face him. "My mother would've agreed to anything I wanted. She only wanted to see me happy."

If her mother could only see her now.

"She'd be proud of you," he told her. "She'd admire you for what you're doing to find the truth."

"If she'd told me the truth years ago, I wouldn't be in this position."

She realized how her words sounded the second they came out. Paisley spun around. "I didn't mean that."

Lucas shrugged. "You did, but it's okay."

"Fine, I did." No need in lying. "But I'm still grateful for all you've done so far. I know you'll get to the truth."

"I appreciate the faith." Lucas stepped in and glanced at the gowns. "Are these all worth thirty-thousand as well?"

Paisley groaned. "No. These are all under ten."

"Still sounds absurd for a dress," he muttered.

She turned back around and zipped the final dress in the protective bag. "Spoken like a true man."

A man who could buy every single dress in her shop and still not feel a dent in his bank account.

"I like that one," he said, pointing to the strapless fitted gown with intricate beading around the waist.

Paisley ran her hand over the bag. "That was my favorite out of the ones she tried on, but I can't tell my customers that. I can only guide them."

"Maybe you should've worn this."

Paisley glared at him. "Are you always going to bring up my wedding attire?"

He chuckled and took a step closer. "Not

always. But when we renew our vows, you can get this one."

Paisley nearly choked on her breath. "Renew our vows? Are you insane?"

Lucas shoved his hands in his pockets as one corner of his mouth quirked up in a naughty grin. "Is our one-year anniversary too soon?"

"We're not renewing our vows. Ever."

Would they even be married in a year? She honestly didn't know if her sanity could hold out that long…or her heart. Yes, she was falling for him, but that didn't mean he felt the same. As much as she wanted this to turn to something real, she couldn't stay married if their union was loveless.

She still had some traditional values, even if she went about things in a nontraditional way.

"You don't want to have a chance to wear the gown of your dreams?" he asked, inching closer.

"Who says I won't have that chance?"

she countered. "If this marriage ends, I want to find love."

Something akin to pain flashed in his eyes, but was just as quickly replaced by desire.

"You keep saying there's an expiration." Lucas reached up and tucked her hair behind her ears, trailing his fingers along her jawline. "I'm starting to think you don't like me around."

On the contrary, she liked having him around too much. And each day that passed only reminded her of what they could've had, what they could've been, had his father not intervened.

But she had nobody else to blame but herself. She should've stood her ground, fought for the life she and Lucas had dreamed of.

Perhaps this was her penance, being in a loveless marriage based on blackmail and revenge. She had to assume that was part of his angle. Revenge on her for leaving him the way she did.

Paisley reached up and eased his hands away from her face.

"Last night changed things," she told him. "I'm not sure where you stand, but you need to know that when you do things for me, and I'm not talking sex, it makes me remember how we were. It makes me remember the dreams we shared and how we never thought anything could come between us."

Lucas remained silent and she had no clue what he was thinking, so she used this momentum bursting through her to continue her honesty.

"When I left you that note before," she started, then swallowed as emotions clogged her throat. "Um..."

Lucas shoved his hands back in his pockets and stepped back. "There's no need to revisit the past."

"Our past has been the third party in this marriage and I think we do need to revisit it," she insisted, because now that she'd started, now that they'd grown closer, she needed him to know. "There's a resentment and anger in you that wasn't there before. I know all of that is my fault. I know I should've handled things differently. But I need you to understand—"

"That you handed me a damn note?" he yelled. "A note, Paisley."

He never called her by her real name unless he was upset. Bringing up their past upset her as well, but until they resurrected that time and talked about it, she didn't know how she could keep going. It was getting too difficult—the emotions, the memories. Her mind screamed at her to keep her distance, to not let this arrangement get any more complicated or emotional. But her heart, well, it had a mind of its own and had never fully closed back up from the gaping hole Lucas had left.

The void had been with her for years and now that she had him back, he filled that spot so perfectly. She'd always known there was nobody else, but how did she manage to hang on to what they had now?

There was so much damage, so many variables out of her control.

She'd hurt him by leaving that note. But he had to understand, she'd ripped her own heart out as well.

"I couldn't do it face-to-face," she cried.

When he only stood there staring at her, Paisley grabbed the last gown and marched from the dressing room. With shaky hands, she hung it back on the rack and attempted to regain her composure.

"I never took you for a coward."

Lucas's low accusation had Paisley gasping and spinning to face him. "Maybe I was a coward, but maybe I was trying to put your needs ahead of my own. I know you don't want to believe that, but I could never forgive myself if I was the reason you didn't go after your dreams."

That bright blue gaze held her. "Did you ever think maybe you were my dream? Did you stop to think that had you told me what happened, I would've found a way to make things work between us? Who says I had to give up anything?"

Maybe bringing up all of this was a mistake. Even after all these years, the hurt wrapped all around her heart, squeezing out every single emotion she'd felt back then.

Paisley had thought discussing old feelings and tending those wounds would help for their present and their future, but clearly she'd made a mistake.

"You know what? Forget it." She held up her hands, admitting defeat because she simply couldn't do this. "I just wanted you to know where I came from. I thought since we were…well, married, that maybe I should try to get you to understand. I can't blame it all on your father for confronting me. I know I made the choice to break things off. But you have to know I did it because I loved you and I was scared."

She started walking by him, but he reached for her arm. Paisley came to a halt, but didn't turn to look at him.

"I didn't come here to fight," he murmured. "I really came to take you out to a nice dinner."

A piece of her heart melted. Maybe they couldn't rehash the past. Maybe at this point, all they could do was focus on who they were now and leave that young couple alone.

What if Lucas wasn't working another angle? What if his sole purpose was to get her to give him a child? Could that be all? Granted that was a huge deal, but he could've turned her away in his office and found another woman to start a family with. A successful, wealthy, sexy man like him would certainly have his choice.

"Where are we going?" she asked, trying to salvage their evening and end an argument.

Lucas smiled and her heart fluttered. "I have a surprise for you."

# Thirteen

"I think these turned out rather great."

Lucas held up the colorful strip of photos and admired them. Well, they were a little off center, but what else did he expect from a shopping mall photo booth?

"Let me see." Paisley laughed as she reached for them. She took one look and laughed even harder. "Half of my face is missing from this one and the bottom picture looks like our mug shots."

He shifted to look over her shoulder. Honestly, he didn't care what they looked like. The intensity of their discussion at the bridal shop had made him change his mind on where they were going. He'd had reservations at his favorite steak house, but they both needed to unwind and do something utterly silly.

So they'd come to the mall.

"We didn't have wedding photos done, so these will have to do."

Paisley snorted. "Why not? Our wedding was tacky anyway, might as well have a photo booth as our photographer."

"These will look great on my desk," he told her, taking the photos back. He slid them into his shirt pocket and grabbed her hand. "Let's go grab something to eat."

"Wait," she said. "You're putting those on your desk?"

With a shrug, he led her toward the food court. "Why wouldn't I? Most people have a photo of their spouse at their office."

"We're not most couples and I don't know anyone who uses a photo booth to get a picture of his loved one."

That stopped him. Lucas kept his hold on her hand, but turned to face her. Love couldn't enter this marriage. At least not from her. She couldn't profess any such thing because, while he might not believe in love, it was clear she did and he didn't want her to be under any illusion that this would develop into what they once had.

Paisley's eyes widened as if she just realized the words she'd uttered. With a shaky smile, she shook her head and kept going.

"You know what I mean," she said in a rush. "I don't actually think you love me, but I'm at least hoping you don't hate me."

Was that what she thought? That he hated her? Despite the hurt he'd felt years ago, even at his darkest time after she'd left, he could never hate her.

Lucas stared at her another minute before turning to face her fully and taking her other hand. People milled about them in the busy area, but he didn't care. This was so much more important.

"I've never hated you," he corrected. "I

wanted to, but I never did. Hate would've been easier to deal with."

Her eyes searched him, as if she wanted to hear more, but he had no more to give. That was all he could divulge about his feelings and still remain in control. The slithering guilt about using her to get to Sterling gnawed at his conscience.

"Well, that's something," she finally murmured. She tipped her chin and smiled. "So, are we really eating here?"

Lucas pushed aside everything outside this moment and let out a fake gasp. "You mean you don't want a salty pretzel with cheese dip or questionable pizza?"

"Hey, I'm always up for junk food. I just didn't think someone like you would eat in a place where you technically serve yourself."

Lucas squeezed her hand and headed toward the pretzel stand. "Did you just call me a snob?"

She fell in step with him and gave him

a nudge with her shoulder. "More like… choosy."

Lucas stepped into the line and sighed. "You know, we may have grown up in a different type of household, but that doesn't mean I think I'm better than anyone and I sure as hell know good food."

Paisley laughed. "I wouldn't call a pretzel that's been sitting in a warmer cube good food."

Lucas pointed to the surrounding concessions. "We'll grab something from each one and then we'll judge whose food is the best."

"Where were you really taking me tonight?" she asked as they moved up in the line. "Because I'm sure you had fancy reservations that required you to wear a jacket and tie."

Which was why he'd shed them in the car before they'd arrived. He'd wanted her relaxed, he'd wanted to see her smile, and he'd figured the mall was probably as far removed as possible from what he had planned at an upscale restaurant.

"Plans change," he replied. "I wanted something simple, maybe like we used to have. There's so much going on. We both needed a break."

The smile she offered was like a punch to his gut, and Lucas wondered if he should've kept the stuffy old reservations. But thankfully the line moved and broke the moment.

They'd only been married a short time, but he realized then that Paisley wasn't that different from the young girl he'd once known.

She might own the poshest bridal boutique in the area, but she was a humble woman with big worries. He didn't want to feel guilty for his actions and he didn't want to get caught up in her again because all of this was so shaky. He had no clue how this was all going to end. At this point, he had to take this marriage like he did all of his cases. One day at a time.

"Maybe we could go to the movies after dinner?" she asked, her smile wide and hopeful.

Yeah, there went that punch to the gut again. Nobody ever affected him like Paisley…and he knew nobody ever would.

"I'm choosing the movie," he replied with a flirty wink. "Just try to keep your hands to yourself if we sit in the back row."

Paisley laughed. "My husband is the handsy one."

"Very true," he agreed. "So you better keep those moans to a minimum."

Paisley set the dish on the table and stood back to survey her work. Lucas had told her he'd be working late on another case he had to wrap up and his cooking duties weren't going to happen tonight. As soon as she'd closed up the boutique, she pulled up her cooking app and headed to the store.

She'd seriously considered re-creating the junk from the mall a few nights ago just as a joke, but opted to make a nice meal instead. He'd been working so hard on not just her case, but those of his other clients. She'd caught him sneaking out of bed in the middle of the night and poring over the rest of the boxes she'd brought from her home. The boxes were the last of her mother's belongings and they'd just been too painful for Paisley to search through.

At first, she'd started going through them, looking for any clue that would lead her toward Sterling, but nothing had stood out and emotions had always consumed her.

Warped as it might sound, Lucas had been amazing during this process and she wanted to show him how much she appreciated his hard work.

So here she stood two hours after getting home from the store, praying she'd managed a meal that was edible. She wanted to impress him, she wanted him to see her as something other than a painful past or a way to grow his lineage.

Damn, that sounded so absurd even in

her own thoughts, but it was true. Part of her wanted him to start to feel more for her…because if she was having all of these feelings emerge, she certainly didn't want to be alone.

Yes, they'd been in love in the past, but that was where all of those emotions remained. Everything she felt now stemmed from the present. Being with him again only showed her that maybe he truly was the one for her. Life and obstacles had pulled them apart, but maybe they were meant to be together. Maybe they needed this growth, these trials to realize just how special they were.

Or maybe she was a complete and utter fool and a hopeless romantic. Lucas didn't believe in love. He'd basically put up an invisible barrier around his heart…not that she could blame him.

The bell sounded from the elevator and the nerves in her belly quickened. So silly. She shouldn't be worried about what he thought; she should be more concerned about him finding the truth about her father. That was the sole reason that led her to his office only a few short weeks ago.

Instead, she glanced to the living room where she'd de-Paisleyed the throw pillows and tried to incorporate more of his boringness.

Wasn't marriage all about balance?

The elevator slid open, and Lucas stepped out. The moment the door closed behind him, he pulled off his black Stetson and hung it on the peg near the door.

Paisley waited until he glanced up and she caught his attention. His eyes scanned the table behind her before he drew his brows in and crossed the penthouse.

"No naked chef tonight?" he asked.

"That was a onetime thing," she admitted. "I'd hate for you to think that was the norm."

"Such a shame." He moved right into her, utterly invading her space and wrapping his arms around her waist. "You didn't have to cook, but I'm glad you did.

I skipped lunch and my last client wanted me to head for drinks after we wrapped up, but I bowed out. I'm beat."

He'd never really discussed his work with her, except that little bit that involved her mother. Maybe he did want to pull her a little more into his world.

"Well, I didn't test it first," she warned, placing her hands on his shoulders. "But I know you like steak, so I went from there."

He gave her a quick kiss on the lips before stepping around her and letting out a low whistle.

"I'm impressed."

"I'd hold back praise until you actually taste it."

Lucas glanced over his shoulder to her. "You went to a good bit of trouble for this meal."

Paisley wasn't great at dealing with compliments of the domestic goddess variety, so she skirted around him and grabbed the bottle of wine from the ice bucket.

"Don't get too excited," she told him as

she poured him a glass of Chianti. "I had to look everything up. It's not like I was raised with a mom who showed me how to make homemade mashed potatoes with gravy or roll out fresh biscuits."

After she served herself some wine, she placed the bottle back in the bucket and risked glancing to Lucas. He remained in place, his eyes locked on her.

"Your mother didn't have to make homemade anything," he stated. "She had other areas she excelled at, I'm sure."

Paisley attempted a smile and started filling the plates. "I've never thought about it before," she told him. "I mean, she did work her butt off to support us. I didn't know any different than having her gone most of the time or there were days I had to go to work with her when she couldn't afford a sitter. By the time I was ten, she just started leaving me alone and would call on her breaks to check in."

Ten years old. Paisley couldn't imagine leaving a ten-year-old home alone, but then again, she wasn't a single parent with limited options. Never once did she doubt her mother's love. The woman just made life choices that made things more difficult at times.

"She never dated," Paisley went on. "Or if she did, I never met the men. It always seemed to just be the two of us. I guess that's why this is so hard. I had no clue she knew who my father was and purposely kept it from me."

Lucas took a seat next to her instead of across from her. Once she sat down, he took her hand and stared into her eyes.

"Maybe she didn't know," he defended. "That's still to be determined and I'm sure we'll find out more once we get proof on Sterling."

Paisley sighed. "Is that even possible at this point? I doubt he would even know unless my mother flat out told him, and if she did tell him, why didn't he claim me or ever reach out?"

Paisley had so many questions and there

were only two people who could answer them: her mother, who was no longer living, and her real father, if he ever knew anything to begin with.

"It's hopeless, isn't it?" she asked.

"I've never given up on a client and I sure as hell am not about to start with my wife."

His conviction had her blossom of hope growing. She truly believed him. She just didn't know how he'd pull this off.

"I just want to go see him," she muttered.

Lucas's fork clattered to his plate a second before he reached for her hand and squeezed. "Patience. That's the one thing you have to have in my business. It's not easy, and can be downright maddening at times. But I promise, we will confront him. Together."

*Together.* Perhaps he did want them to be a team and maybe in more ways than just this case. Having dinner together every night seemed so familial and they'd settled right into a nice pattern.

Paisley couldn't help but feel that maybe

this could work. She so badly wanted to tell him her true feelings, but she needed to be patient. Isn't that what he'd just told her?

Every part of her life now required the right timing—confronting Sterling and telling Lucas she'd fallen in love with him again.

# Fourteen

Lucas had never been the best at sleeping all night. Clients and cases would wake him, and his mind never fully seemed to shut down.

Which was why he sat on the floor of his living room with another open box of Lynette's things. She wasn't the most organized person. He'd uncovered some planners that she seemed to have good intentions of completing. She'd start out the year with detailed accounts of events, only to taper off about May or June.

Nothing in any of those pointed toward any man, let alone Sterling. It truly did look like all she did was work and spend time with Paisley.

He pulled out a planner dated for the year Paisley would've been four. Lucas still flipped through each page, even knowing the end of the year would be blank, as per the usual, and found a set of pockets in the back.

Shifting in his seated position, Lucas turned toward the rustic coffee table and searched the pockets. A coupon fell out, overlooked bills and an envelope with a name on it. Jeb Smith. Lucas pulled out the folded piece of paper.

Jeb,
You are behind on your child support AGAIN! Why do I have to always remind you of this? It's bad enough you're her father and have dismissed her, but you could at least send what you owe so

I can raise her without worrying about two or three jobs.

Don't think I won't contact an attorney if you keep ignoring me. You're six months behind now. Pay up!

Lucas read the letter through a second and third time.

What the hell? Who was Jeb Smith? Why did Lynette never mail this? Clearly she was angry and obviously needed the money.

Lucas glanced over his shoulder toward the bedroom where Paisley slept. If this Jeb turned out to be her father, that would destroy any thoughts of Sterling.

So many mixed emotions swirled around inside him at this revelation. If Sterling was out of the picture, that meant Lucas wouldn't get his revenge through Paisley. But more importantly, she wouldn't have the Perry name. That sounded so selfish even to him, but if Paisley were a Perry, she would've had sisters and possibly a brother, if Roarke was actually Sterling's son.

If this letter, pointing toward Jeb Smith, proved to be truthful, Lucas had a sinking feeing he'd just found Paisley's biological father.

He quickly put everything back in the planner, keeping the letter and envelope to himself. After placing everything back in the box, Lucas came to his feet and stretched until his back popped. He really should get to bed, but this development had him more wired than ever to uncover the truth for Paisley.

Somewhere along the way this case shifted from pure revenge to wanting to do this for the woman he still cared about. Oh, he still wanted Sterling to pay for every crime he'd committed, but now he wanted Paisley to find that family she deserved.

What she didn't deserve was being kept in the dark, but that was exactly what he needed to do until he found Mr. Smith and talked to him.

Lucas went to the kitchen and made a cup of coffee. This was going to be a long night and an even longer day if he uncovered the location of this new player in the game.

He took the coffee to his office and closed the door. In no time he had his laptop up and was on the hunt. It didn't take long for him to find several Jeb Smiths in Texas, considering the first and last name were quite popular.

He was successful at his job for a reason and by six in the morning, after two more cups of coffee and before Paisley woke, Lucas had an address and he was just thankful Jeb was only in the next town over and alive and well.

He'd go pay him a visit, take this letter and Lynette's picture, and hopefully get the answers Paisley deserved.

And once Lucas had all the facts, he'd present them to her. Then they could decide what to do about this marriage. A sinking pit in his stomach had him wondering if she'd follow through with ending things or if she'd stay. While Lucas tried to remain emotionally distant, he couldn't deny he'd started developing more feelings for her than he would've liked.

He hadn't been able to avoid that heart tug years ago and now was no different. Having her in his bed every night, knowing how determined she was to remain on her feet and find the truth, seeing her passion for her work all made him realize the girl he'd wanted all those years ago had grown into the woman he didn't want to live without.

If she walked out again, Lucas wasn't sure he could handle the void again. All the more reason to never tell her how he truly felt.

Paisley turned side to side in the mirror and smoothed down her red cocktail dress. Lucas had planned on coming to Melinda's party, but he'd texted a few hours ago and said he was following a lead and couldn't get back in time. He told her to go enjoy herself and he'd meet her back at home.

When she'd asked if the lead was on her case, he never replied.

Paisley didn't want to go to the party. She wanted to wait and see what was going on because his silence spoke volumes. He'd been so up-front with her so far, she had to believe everything he was doing was in her best interest.

She hoped the truth revealed itself soon. She was on the brink of telling him she loved him. There was only so long she could hold in her emotions and he deserved to know where she stood.

Plus, he loved the color red.

Paisley had chosen this slinky dress with her husband in mind. She'd imagined him slipping her out of this as soon as they made it back to the penthouse, or maybe he'd try in the elevator on the way up. Or maybe he'd give her another one of those toe-curling massages.

With one last glance to her hair and a

swipe of pale shimmer gloss to her lips, Paisley grabbed her gold clutch and headed to the elevator. Lucas had ordered his driver to take Paisley to the party even though she insisted she could drive herself.

Arguing with that man was sometimes just a losing battle. But when he was being adorably sweet, she couldn't quite fault him.

The drive to Melinda's home didn't take long, but Paisley found herself looking at her phone, waiting for any update or clue as to what he'd found.

Paisley thanked the driver as he assisted her from the car, and he informed her he'd be out here waiting whenever she was ready to go. No doubt by her husband's orders.

This was a whole new lifestyle for her— living in a penthouse that was three times the size of her little town house, having a driver at her disposal, being made love to the way Lucas made love to her and having someone put her needs first.

There was no way Paisley could leave. She wanted to build a life with him; she wanted to give him that family he wanted. She had so much in her to give because when she'd left him all those years ago, she'd never given her heart to another man. There had been no one that even came close to Lucas.

Yes, he was harder now, more cautious, but that all stemmed from having been hurt. She'd made a mistake and she knew building anything new would take time... time she was more than willing to give because she'd already created their little family in her mind.

After this party, Paisley would tell him she loved him. She would tell him she wanted to move forward with a real marriage, a real family. He may not be ready to admit love yet, and that was fine. But she wasn't going anywhere, and he could take his time in coming to grips with his emotions.

With a renewed hope for her future, Paisley headed toward the limestone condo high-rise. The doorman greeted her, and the attendant at the elevator happily sent her on up to the twenty-fourth floor. Melinda and her sister Angela both lived in this stunning building, but on different floors. Paisley had to assume Angela would be at the party, too, and perhaps their other sister, Esme.

Nerves of anticipation curled low in her belly. These women could potentially be her half sisters. If Lucas came back with information confirming Sterling was her father, Paisley would have names to put with her new family.

What would it be like to have sisters?

The elevator opened on Melinda's floor and Paisley made her way to the condo unit. She'd barely knocked when the door swung wide and the hostess herself beamed a wide smile.

"You made it," Melinda exclaimed. "Come on in. Where's your husband?"

*Trying to see if you and I share a father.*

"He's away on business," Paisley replied.

She stepped into the suite and glanced around at the people mingling as trays of delicate finger foods passed by in the deft hands of uniformed waitstaff.

"Well, I'm glad you could make it anyway," Melinda stated. "Come out to the balcony. Esme and Angela are out there and I know they'd love to see you."

Paisley slid her clutch beneath her arm and followed Melinda out to the balcony, which overlooked Houston. The lights from the city were the perfect picturesque backdrop for the cocktail party.

"Paisley," Esme squealed. "It's so great to see you again."

The beautiful blonde stepped forward and gave a half hug so as not to spill her champagne glass.

"Great to see you," Paisley replied, smiling.

"Excuse me," Melinda said. "I'm going to grab you a drink."

Melinda stepped inside and plucked a

fluted glass from a server's tray and returned, handing it to Paisley.

"I'm so glad you could come," Angela
chimed in, sipping her own glass. "And
that red dress is killer!"

"It's a shame Lucas isn't here with you,"
Melinda joked. "But maybe it's a good
thing. No man could resist that."

"Lucas?" Esme asked, her brows drawn
in. "Lucas Ford?"

Paisley smiled and gripped the stem of
her glass. "Yes."

"Her new husband," Melinda added.

Angela's eyes darted to Paisley's hand,
then back up. "It's a good thing he didn't
come," she murmured.

"Excuse me?" Paisley asked.

"Getting him in a room full of Perrys is
probably not the best idea," Esme added.
"He has had a thing for our dad for years."

Paisley stared at the women, stunned by
what she heard, but trying to process everything. Lucas hated Sterling that much?
A hatred that spanned years and he'd failed

to say one word to her when she first approached him?

No, that couldn't be right. He wouldn't hide something like that from her.

"I forgot about that," Melinda said, clearly surprised. "I mean, I knew Lucas hated Dad, but I didn't put it all together when you said you guys had married. I was just so happy for you. He still would've been welcome here."

"Of course," Angela added. "Lucas is a nice guy and his reputation is impeccable. But I'm not sure he would've liked it very much or felt comfortable here."

Paisley remained silent, confused, hurt, wondering if this was true. She wanted to believe him, she'd put so much faith in him. Lucas hadn't said a word when she'd told him whose party she was attending. Not. One. Word.

Surely this was all wrong information or gossip.

"You didn't know this, did you?" Melinda asked, sympathy lacing her tone.

Paisley took a sip of her drink, mostly to have something to do and to help push down that lump of emotions and doubt that clogged her throat.

"No, I wasn't aware," she admitted, suddenly feeling nauseated. "We were apart for years, so we both have things in our past that haven't come out yet."

Like the fact she'd never stopped loving him and he opted to deceive. Oh, she prayed that wasn't the truth, but the niggling in the back of her mind said she had to be realistic.

"Apparently our dad did something to Lucas's father years ago," Angela added. "I don't know all the details, but I do know Lucas has made it clear he's not a friend of the Perrys."

The women continued to discuss, reminding each other of what their father had indeed done to Lucas's. Something about a business deal gone wrong, lies, betrayal... all of that sounded like Sterling, and Paisley wasn't doubting all of that had happened.

What she was doubting, however, was her husband's devotion to her. If all this was true, was Lucas using her as a stepping-stone to get closer to Sterling and serve justice for his father's wrongdoings?

The idea made her tremble—out of fear, anger, the unknown.

Paisley's cell vibrated in her clutch beneath her arm. She'd been waiting for Lucas to get back to her. Could that be him now? Had he found the truth he'd been looking for?

"Paisley, I drove by your shop earlier and that is a gorgeous strapless gown in the window," Melinda stated, obviously trying to turn the conversation around. "If I marry, I want that one."

Paisley attempted a smile. "I will be happy to set you up. You would make a stunning bride."

"I just want to come in and try everything on," Esme said with a laugh. "Your shop is so elegant and every wedding you've done that I've been to has been like a fairy tale."

"I love my job and I hope every bride feels special when she's there."

Paisley did not want to stand around and make small talk, not even when the chatter involved her beloved boutique. She wanted to make haste and get back home. She wanted to know if Lucas had deceived her purposefully. If he'd married her only as a way to seek the ultimate revenge.

But if she left now, the ladies would know why and she really didn't want anyone to have an insight into her sham of a marriage.

As much as this bombshell hurt, she wanted to hash it out in private with Lucas and at least give him a chance to defend himself. It would be so easy to rush into judgment and lay into him about how much it hurt that he hadn't told her about his hatred for Sterling.

But she wanted to hear his side because she prayed he hadn't married her as some warped way to get revenge on Sterling for doing his father wrong…and for her leaving him years ago.

# Fifteen

After about an hour, Paisley couldn't stand any more small talk. She checked her phone, seeing a message from Lucas, and feigned a need to get home.

The ladies assumed she was just in a hurry to get home to her husband, but her reasons for rushing home were far removed from what they were winking and hinting at.

Paisley took the elevator and rushed out the front door. She didn't have to say a word to the driver. He had been standing next to the car and immediately opened the back door for her so she could slide in.

She settled back against the seat and glanced at Lucas's text again. He'd simply said he was home and he'd wait up for her, but hoped she was having fun. There was no mention of his findings, nothing that hinted as to what he'd been doing.

Paisley tried to relax her breathing, to calm herself so she didn't just go in and explode all over him. She truly did want to give him a chance to defend himself.

The idea that she was a pawn in his grand scheme to get to Sterling sickened her. After all they'd been through in the past, all they'd been through just in the past few weeks, she didn't want to believe the worst.

The car pulled in front of Lucas's condo building, and Paisley didn't wait on the driver. The car had barely rolled to a stop before she jerked the door handle and bolted out. She headed into the building and typed in the code at the elevator with shaky hands. When the doors opened, she clutched her purse to still her nerves and watched the numbers light up as she ascended to the penthouse.

The moment the doors slid open, Paisley pulled in a deep breath and stepped into the suite, placing her clutch on the table next to the elevator. Lucas came from the hallway, his hair a mess from his hat, his shirt unbuttoned, sleeves rolled up on his forearms. There was a wariness to his heavy-lidded gaze, but he offered her a smile that never failed to curl all around her heart.

"Had I known you were going out looking so sexy, I would've made sure I was back in time." He reached her and slid his hands up her bare arms. "Red is your color."

When he started to pull her in, Paisley flattened her palms against his chest and took a step back. Suspicion quickly replaced the exhaustion.

"Something wrong?" he asked.

"Where were you today?"

He stared at her for a moment, then shook his head and raked a hand over the back of his neck.

"I was working," he murmured. "There's something you need to know."

Paisley's heart quickened as nerves like she'd never known consumed her. She knew. She knew before she even opened her mouth, but she had to hear him say it.

"Does this have anything to do with your revenge against Sterling?"

Lucas didn't flinch, he didn't look surprised, he didn't even attempt to deny the allegation. The truth settled heavily between them.

"My work today had to do with you," he stated, as if that explained all the missing pieces he'd conveniently kept from her.

"Which I'm sure just pushes your agenda to bring justice to Sterling."

Lucas nodded, a dark look clouding his eyes. "I hate the man. He ruined my father's business and I won't apologize for seeking justice or for trying to honor my father."

Paisley let out a humorless laugh. "You must've really loved it when I stepped into your office and wanted you to research him. I just handed you a golden ticket to get the ultimate revenge if I was his daughter."

He stared at her for another minute before blowing out a sigh and turning from her, muttering something beneath his breath.

Paisley watched as he paced in front of the wall of living room windows. The dark night behind him only added to the mystery of this man. The man she'd thought she'd known so well...but she'd been so blinded by love. Or was it foolishness? At this point, weren't they the same emotion?

Maybe that was what sickened her most. She'd wanted to believe there was no hidden agenda. She'd wanted to believe that when he'd said he wanted a child, that maybe that was the only stipulation.

Like a damn fool, she'd been ready to

give everything to him. Her heart, her life, her future.

Lucas had his back to her, staring out into the night. She wanted to know what was going through his mind, but at the same time, she didn't know if he'd just spout off more lies and keep the real truth hidden like he'd been doing.

"Sterling is a bastard and, yes, I did see you as a way to get back at him if you turned out to be his daughter."

He turned to face her, shoving his hands in his pockets. "But so much changed between us and... Damn it. He's not your father."

Paisley heard the words, attempted to process them, but could she believe anything he said at this point? How could he be so sure about Sterling? Who had he spoken to?

She had so many questions, but would he give her the answers she wanted, the ones she deserved?

On shaky legs, Paisley made her way

across the room and rested her hands on the back of the leather chair. As much as she felt she needed to take a seat, she wanted to look like she was strong, in control—though she felt anything but.

"Why should I believe you?" she asked.

"I've been going through the boxes you've brought," he started. "I searched through some of Lynette's old planners last night and another letter slipped out. She wrote it to a Jeb Smith, but never mailed it. The letter said—"

"I want to see it," she demanded, barely holding her emotions together.

"Paisley—"

"Now."

Lucas stared at her a minute before he crossed the room toward her and pulled a folded paper from his pocket. Without a word he handed it over. Paisley attempted to calm her breathing and will her hands to stop shaking before she opened the note. Anything inside here was clearly going to alter her future, and now that it came down to it, she wasn't sure if she was ready to know the truth.

Carefully, she unfolded the letter and read each word her mother had written. The emotions flooded her from so many angles. Seeing her mother's beautiful cursive writing had a knot of loss forming in her gut. But Paisley pushed through that pain as she experienced another round from the fact this Jeb Smith could be her father.

Paisley had never heard that name in her life, but from the way her mother demanded child support, Paisley wondered if this was real. At this point, she wasn't sure if even her mother knew who the father was.

The only thing that was clear now was that Lucas had lied to her and that hurt more than not knowing the truth about her father.

"I don't believe this or you," she stated,

refolding the paper and tossing it into the chair in front of her. "Sterling makes sense. He's the type of guy my mother would've gravitated toward and he's already been rumored to have had affairs."

The muscle in Lucas's jaw ticked, his lips thinned. "He's not your father. I went to see Jeb today and he was fully aware of you. He even had photos of you as a child. Apparently Lynette had given them to him."

Paisley's vision wavered. Black dots swam before her. She shook her head, gripping the seat back and closing her eyes. There was a man out there who knew he was her father…and hadn't sought her out. There was a man her mother had known for sure and hadn't said a word about to Paisley.

The emotions were too strong, her heart too raw to attempt to process what all of this meant. Had anyone in her life been truthful? It hit her then, hard, that she truly was alone.

Lucas reached out to her and his hand

rested on her arm. Paisley jerked away as she focused on him.

"Don't touch me," she murmured.

The last thing she wanted was attention out of pity. She was alone, right? There was no need to lean on someone who was just using her. She would get through all of this, somehow, and come out stronger.

But first she needed to go home, be by herself and have a much-needed break-down.

"You looked like you were about to pass out on me."

She rubbed at her temples, then shoved her hair from her face. "I don't need your help with anything anymore. Not the truth, not my health, nothing."

The light glinted off the rock on her hand and Paisley wasted no time twisting the bands off. She held them out, but Lucas merely glanced at them and back up to her.

"They're yours."

Paisley laughed. "I don't want them. Save them for the next woman you use or return them. I don't give a damn, but they will not be leaving with me."

Lucas shook his head. "You're not leaving."

Backing up a step, Paisley let out a mock laugh. "Like hell I'm not. If this Jeb Smith is my father, then we're done. I told you from the beginning that this wasn't permanent."

Yeah, she'd said those words, but she'd ignored them and had fallen face-first in love. She hadn't taken her own advice and had totally ignored all the red flags as to why getting too emotionally attached was a bad idea.

So here she was. Brokenhearted, barely holding herself together, and the daughter of a man she'd never heard of…and clearly a man who wanted nothing to do with her since he'd known of her existence.

Paisley bit her quivering lip and turned away. She did not need a witness to her vulnerability and agony.

"Paisley, don't shut me out," Lucas

pleaded. "I wanted to find all the facts before I came to you. I was trying to make this process as painless as possible."

She whirled back around, swiping at the tear that had the nerve to escape. "What process? Finding my father or you lying to my face night after night as we made love? Did you even feel guilty for using me? After all we shared before, after what we were building now, where the hell was your conscience in all of this? Because I would never use someone I love."

His brows rose as he stared back at her without a word.

"That's right. I love you." Another tear escaped and she didn't bother wiping it away. She wanted him to see the damage he'd caused. "At least when I broke your heart years ago, I did it so you'd have a better life. I did it because I loved you so much. I never lied to you, not one time."

Lucas pursed his lips and gave a clipped nod. He glanced away, but not before Paisley saw a shimmer in his eyes.

Could he actually have a heart, after all?

"I won't be staying here," she told him. "I'll come back and get my things and my mother's boxes when you're at work. My attorney will be in touch regarding the divorce."

His eyes darted right back to hers. "Don't make any decisions out of anger. We need to talk about this."

"We've been talking," she reminded him. "The story won't change. You lied to me and used me. I thought we could actually have something together again. I was foolish enough to want to give you that family you mentioned. I was hopeful that you'd grow to love me again and maybe this would all work out. But that was all too naive and I can see exactly what this is and what this isn't."

She started to turn, but he reached for her.

"At least let me tell you about your real father," he stated. "You have his face shape and the same mouth, the same dimple to the right of your lips."

Paisley stared down at her gold, strappy sandals on the glossy hardwood floors. She didn't want to look at him, didn't want him to see the impact of everything he said.

"He never wanted children," Lucas went on. "He was paying your mother at first for child support, but then he got laid off from his job in construction. He kept telling her to just move on and leave him out of it. He thought you'd be better off without him as a father. Surely you can understand that."

Paisley didn't miss his hint at the similarities between this man thinking she was better off without him and her doing the same to Lucas years ago.

But this wasn't the same. This wasn't some young love trying to figure out their future. This was her life, her past, the part that shaped her into who she was today.

"You can text me all of his information and I'll take it from here," she told him, heading to the elevator. She grabbed her clutch and hit the button. "My lawyer will contact you this week."

She didn't turn around, didn't want to look into his eyes again. The pain she felt... She couldn't even put a label on such emotions, but she didn't want him to see. Yes, she'd wanted him to know he'd hurt her, but now that pain bordered on soul crushing and heartbreaking, and she didn't want to be seen as weak.

The doors slid open and she fully expected him to call out her name, to come up behind her and try to convince her to stay. But the doors slid open and Paisley stepped in.

The second she turned, her eyes locked with his. Damn it. She hadn't wanted him to be the last thing she saw as she left.

But maybe this was what she needed to finalize this chapter on her life. The anguish on his face almost had her pausing, but no. He was good at manipulating people, manipulating her. If he had pain or angst, that was all on him.

She had her own life to piece back together. As much as she still loved him, she just didn't have the energy to play this marriage game any longer.

# Sixteen

Silence was deafening.

Lucas had heard the term before, but never fully comprehended those words until Paisley walked out of his penthouse.

That had been five hours ago.

Lucas stared out into the night from his living room. He still held on to the tumbler of bourbon he'd poured an hour ago. He had no clue what to do, how to be. He wasn't himself without Paisley and he'd severed any chance of having her in his life.

But he had no heart to give her. One time

he'd thought he had, but he wouldn't have treated her this way if he'd truly loved her. Using her had been a mistake, but for years he'd hated Sterling and the second she stepped into his office, Lucas had seen a clever way in.

What he hadn't seen was the woman he'd loved once, the woman who'd had the ability to hurt him. Instead, he'd seen anger and resentment.

He was a damn fool.

Lucas stared down at the glass in his hand and had every desire to throw it and hear the shatter, but that would solve nothing. Who the hell was he angry at? He was the only one who'd made a mess of this entire ordeal.

But he'd found the answers for Paisley. That was most important. After all she'd been through, she deserved to know the truth.

He hadn't gotten a chance to tell her that her biological father was sick, but from here on out, that part of her life was out of his hands. He'd texted her the information she'd wanted and had gotten no reply—not that he expected one.

Lucas turned from the view that had once been lit up with lights from the city, but now, in the middle of the night, was mostly dark. There was probably some correlation between that and his life, but right now he couldn't figure it out.

He took the glass to the bar and headed toward the bedroom. The second he stepped through the doorway, he realized his mistake. He couldn't sleep in here. Paisley was everywhere. Her satin robe draped across the bottom of the bed, her heels placed near the closet where she'd stepped out of them yesterday, the perfume…damn. That floral scent was everywhere.

Lucas stared at the bed they'd been sleeping in and knew he wouldn't be back in this room for a long, long time.

He marched across to the other side of the penthouse, unbuttoning his shirt as he went. One of the guest rooms would have to do. Maybe he wouldn't see her there, maybe he'd sleep, maybe he'd actually be able to move on without her.

But he knew the truth. Paisley had infiltrated his life on two separate occasions and both times when she'd walked out, he'd been left feeling completely gutted with no hope of what tomorrow would bring.

Paisley stared across the street at the simple bungalow owned by Jeb Smith. She'd barely slept last night because she'd been so nervous about today and confronting the man who supposedly was her father.

Though if she was being honest with herself, she couldn't sleep because she'd been back in her town house, alone in her bed and trying to get the ache in her heart to subside.

But she couldn't think about Lucas right now. Not that he was ever fully out of her thoughts, but she had to push him to the back. This day was too important. The man inside that house could truly be her father.

Inside her heart, she knew he was. Lucas wouldn't have told her if he wasn't 100 percent certain. Yes, he'd lied to her about Sterling to try to seek his own revenge, but Paisley couldn't question this.

She gripped her door handle and stepped from her car. Pulling in a deep breath, she smoothed down her maxidress and glanced both ways before setting off across the street. Maybe she should've worn jeans. Was a dress too formal? What did one wear to meet a parent for the first time?

Nerves curled all through her, sending doubts shooting off in all directions. There was no turning back. She wanted to know, she deserved to know. She'd already lost one parent and she wanted the opportunity to get to know the other.

She had no clue why her mother hadn't just come out and told her who her father was or why she didn't state his name in the letter. Perhaps she was trying to save him after all this time or maybe she was ashamed of her past. Paisley truly had no idea and she might never know her mother's reasoning. All she knew was she was about to meet her father at long last.

Paisley climbed the porch steps and glanced to the homey wooden swing on the opposite end. With a shaky finger, she pressed the doorbell and stepped back to wait.

The click of a lock and twist of the handle had her pasting on a smile and ready to face whomever was on the other side of that door.

A middle-aged man with silver hair and kind eyes stood on the other side of the glass door. The second his gaze locked with hers, his brows shot up, his mouth dropped in surprise. He quickly opened the door.

"Paisley?" he asked, his tone laced with uncertainty.

She nodded, trying not to let her emotions get the best of her. "Jeb Smith?"

He didn't confirm as he gestured her to come in. "I thought after your husband came by, you might follow."

Paisley stepped into the foyer and stood awkwardly as he closed the door behind her. When he turned to face her once again, he smiled and a piece of her fear melted away.

"Come in and sit down," he told her. "I—I don't even know what to say or…maybe I should get you something to drink?"

Paisley laughed. "I'm fine. I'd say we're both nervous."

He stared at her another minute before shaking his head and blowing out a sigh. "You've grown into such a beautiful young lady."

"It's been a long time since someone called me a young lady," she replied with a slight laugh. "But thank you."

He pointed toward the arched doorway. "Let's go into the living room."

She stepped into the cozy space and took a seat on the sofa as Jeb carefully eased himself into a worn recliner. Paisley's fears returned.

"Are you all right?"

His eyes snapped to hers.

"Sorry," she added. "It's none of my business."

"Don't be sorry," he stated, resting his arms on the edge of the chair. "As I told Lucas, I have a heart issue that's messed up my way of living. I'm tired easy. I have a caregiver that comes in a few times a week to help around the house and get my meds. I'm just…not quite as spry as I used to be."

Heart issue? Paisley crossed her ankles and leaned forward in her seat.

"What can I do to help?"

Jeb shook his head. "Unless you're a miracle worker, there's nothing that can be done. I'm…terminal."

"That can't be," she cried. "I just found you."

Then she remembered what all Lucas had said.

"But you knew about me all along, didn't you?"

Jeb nodded. "I did. Lynette and I weren't necessarily a couple. We dated a few times, but never anything serious. I kept getting laid off work so when she said she was pregnant, I did what I could financially, but it wasn't much. I'd hoped she'd find someone who could provide for you both, but she never did."

"You didn't want me, though." The words hurt, but she came here for answers.

"I wasn't fit to be a father," he corrected. "I'm old enough now to realize I made mistakes where you were concerned. I thought Lynette would find someone and start a real family. I guess I thought if I just paid her what I could and left her alone, you both would be better off."

Paisley listened to him, and had she read this in a letter or email, she'd be furious and assume he was merely making lame excuses. But she heard the remorse in his voice. She could tell by the way he looked at her that he had regrets.

She had a few of her own.

"If I had to do it over, I'd fight to see you, to be part of your life," he added.

"Lucas said you had photos of me," Paisley said.

Jeb nodded. "Your mother would give me pictures every now and then. When I came with a check she would give me one. I only have a few. I...wasn't the best father figure and she had every right to hate me."

Paisley crossed her legs and smoothed her dress down. "Why didn't you get in touch with me in later years?"

"I was ashamed, embarrassed, afraid." He shrugged and glanced out the window as if gathering his thoughts. "I'd say you were about fifteen when I really thought about approaching you, but then I figured you and Lynette were set in your ways. If she hadn't told you about me, there was a reason. I couldn't just come waltzing in and blow up the only world you knew. Then after she passed away..."

His focus came back to her. "I wasn't sure you'd want anything to do with me. I had no clue what she ever told you about your father and I didn't want to disrupt your life."

He might have had a terrible excuse when she'd been young, but as time went on, Paisley fully believed he'd stayed away out of shame and fear.

"Maybe we could have a relationship now," she suggested.

Jeb smiled, the gesture crinkling the corners of his eyes and enhancing the deep lines around his mouth.

"There's nothing I'd like more," he told her. "I hate that I'm sick, that we may not have years left. I've missed a lifetime."

Paisley's throat clogged with emotions, but she truly wanted to be strong for him. "Then we'll have to cram in a lifetime of memories in the time we have."

His smile widened. "Do you have dinner plans?"

Finally, hope spread through her. "I'm having dinner with my dad."

# Seventeen

Lucas stared at the computer screen, but the words kept blurring. He'd been focused on the same sentence for the past hour and he was getting absolutely nowhere.

His cases were not taking top priority like they always had. He couldn't focus, couldn't sleep, couldn't function, because his entire world had blown up and he was wading through the bits and pieces trying to find his new normal.

And if this was it, he wasn't going to make it.

The penthouse was too quiet, so he'd been staying in his office. But on his desk sat the mall photos they'd had done in the photo booth and he couldn't stop staring at them.

He and Paisley looked so ridiculously happy—like the couple they'd once been.

Lucas pushed away from his desk and came to his feet. He shoved his hands in his pockets and glared down at the photo mocking him. This was what he could've had, this was what he'd thrown away all for the sake of revenge.

Now he was left with no revenge and no wife. Well, she was technically his wife until the divorce was finalized. He hadn't heard from her attorney and she'd left his home four days ago.

Four damn days. The longest days of his life.

If he thought he'd been crushed and broken the first time she walked out, that was nothing compared to this time. Both occasions had not been her fault, but she'd been pushed out just the same. Both instances she'd trusted him, confided in him…loved him.

Lucas's eyes started to burn and he blinked as he glanced away from the pictures. Apologizing didn't seem to be enough. How could the words *I'm sorry* cover a multitude of sins?

But he couldn't go on like this. He couldn't go on without her or let her walk out of his life again, because he knew this time would be for good.

Lucas closed out the case he was reading on his computer and sent an email to one of his top guys to take over. The company wouldn't suffer—he'd spent too long making a reputation for himself, but he couldn't put himself on any job right now and give it his all.

The only job he wanted was that of husband to Paisley Ford. She hadn't actually changed her name, but damn it, he liked the sound of it. He wanted to be married to her, for real, without any pretenses or lies.

He wanted to build that life they'd dreamed of so long ago. He wanted kids with her, not just because he wanted a child to pass his legacy to, but because he wanted children with the woman he loved more than the world.

A viselike grip clenched his heart. There was nothing he wouldn't do to win Paisley back. Nothing he wouldn't sacrifice, including his pride. His life meant nothing without her. Even if he'd gotten the revenge he wanted on Sterling, it would have been an empty victory because he'd lost Paisley and she took precedence over everything else.

He scooped up his keys and headed out the back office door. His driver had taken Paisley home the other night and Lucas had ordered the guy to hang around since then for anything she needed.

Lucas couldn't believe she hadn't texted to tell him to back off, but perhaps she was that angry she didn't even want to talk. Or maybe she was using the driver, who knew.

There was nothing Lucas wouldn't give her to make her life easier. He somehow had to get her to understand his actions, and that he'd cared for her, even though he had a poor way of showing it.

Lucas climbed into his SUV and headed toward her town house. He wasn't giving her a heads-up; he didn't want her to make excuses to leave or talk him out of not coming. He needed to see her, needed to just tell his side. Hell, he'd beg, plead, sell his soul to get her back.

He wasn't too proud to admit he'd been a bastard. He wasn't too proud to lay his heart on the line for the woman that he loved. Once he put everything out there, he'd respect her enough to back away and let her think. Walking away would kill him, but he had to let her come to him on her own if that was what she decided.

Baring his heart, laying it before her, and then walking away and leaving all control to her was going to be pure hell. But nothing could be worse than not having her at all.

Four days was too long to be without his wife. It was time to reclaim his life, *their* life, and find a way to make things right.

Sundays were meant for relaxing, but Paisley felt anything but relaxed.

She'd received an insane amount of money in her business account, more than enough to order any dress she'd ever want in her shop, more than enough to pay off her building, and more than enough if she wanted to throw a new car into the mix.

So how could she relax when her soon-to-be ex-husband was trying to buy his way back into her life?

Not that she wasn't thankful for the exorbitant amount of money, but she couldn't keep it. She was filing for divorce and she wasn't going to take something that wasn't hers...the money or the man.

Paisley tightened the belt on her robe and started to head to the master bedroom for a shower when her doorbell rang. Who on earth would be here on a Sunday morning? She didn't just get drop-in visitors and she certainly hadn't invited anyone over. With the mood she'd been in, she tried to keep to herself for fear of lashing out at anyone who asked how she was doing.

She'd had to save every bit of patience and smiles for her customers. Today, though, she'd wanted to do absolutely nothing. She wanted to give her mind time to rest, her heart time to heal, but none of that would happen anytime soon.

She'd never gotten over Lucas when she'd left him years ago—how the hell did she think she'd get over him after becoming his wife and spending every night in his bed?

Paisley smoothed her bed head away from her face as she padded barefoot to the front door. From the silhouette she could make out through the etched glass, she knew exactly who stood on the other side.

Well, it took him long enough and he'd

better be here groveling and down on his knees. Not that she'd take him back. She was going to be strong, stand her ground and not let anyone take advantage of her again.

But she wasn't going to turn down an apology. Tears would help, too. At least she'd know she wasn't in the land of misery alone.

Did he even cry? She'd never seen him show such emotions or anything really other than passion and greed.

No, that wasn't true. He'd shown so much more, but right now, anger and pain fueled her thoughts.

The doorbell chimed again, followed by a knock.

"Tart, I know you're in there."

Damn that nickname.

Paisley flicked the lock on the door and swung it open. Taking in his rumpled hair, his wrinkled shirt that looked like it was from yesterday and the dark circles beneath his eyes, she couldn't help but feel a little sorry for him.

"You look like hell."

Well, that was not exactly what she'd meant to say, but it was the truth. She'd never seen him so frazzled and forlorn, but he'd brought everything upon himself...so why did she feel bad?

"I've been sleeping in my office and I can't focus on work," he told her. "I don't deserve five minutes of your time, but I'm asking for it anyway."

Not only had she never seen him look like this, she'd never heard that tone before. Oh, he still had a strength to his words, but the underlying vibe was definitely broken.

Still, after all he'd put her through, she refused to go easy on him. Why should she? She'd put herself out there from the second she'd walked into his office and he'd taken advantage without even an ounce of guilt. Well, he probably had guilt once he got caught, but he'd slept with her night after night. At any point he could've told her about his father and Sterling.

But he chose to keep her in the dark and continue the lie.

"I know you want to slam that door in my face," he went on. "Do what you have to do, but I'm just asking for a chance to explain my actions. Just like I gave you the chance to explain yours about what happened years ago."

"I call bullshit on that." Paisley gripped the doorknob and seriously thought about slamming the door as he suggested. "You didn't let me fully explain. I attempted and you brushed it aside as a maybe truth because you didn't want to believe your father would lie to you. That hurts, doesn't it? Knowing someone you love, someone you trust with your entire life has betrayed you?"

"I believe what happened with my dad," he told her. "I know you loved me then and I know you love me now. Can I just have five minutes?"

"I think you need quite a bit longer than that to offer a proper apology." She pursed her lips and considered, though her heart was breaking and she wanted to ignore all the red flags and invite him in...straight to her bed. "You have four and a half minutes. Go."

"Can I come in?"

She shifted her stance and leaned against the door. "No."

He stared at her for a minute before he finally nodded and glanced down to his feet. For the first time in her life she wondered if he'd ever been in this position before. He had no control and they both knew it.

Lucas raised his head and focused back on her as his shoulders squared and eyes held hers. "I messed up. There's really no way to sugarcoat that and I want you to know that I'm not here just because I want a child or I want to keep up this arrangement we had. I'm here because I want you back for good. I want a real wedding, I want a real future, no secrets. I want everything with you, Paisley."

She listened, trying to ignore the pull of her heartstrings, but how could she? Each word sounded so heartfelt, not rehearsed at all. Still…

"It's not that simple," she explained. "You can't just come here because you're lonely. You're supposed to hurt. That's your punishment."

He took a step closer, sliding a hand around the dip in her waist and making her shiver. Damn that man for making her feel when she tried so hard not to.

"I'm not here because I hurt," he murmured, staring into her eyes. "I'm here because you're hurt."

Tears pricked her eyes. Why did he know the right words? Why did he have so much charm that he made it impossible for her to hate him?

Paisley blinked back the unshed tears. "Yes, I'm hurting," she admitted. "But words won't just make that pain go away.

I've never been used before, Lucas. And I never thought I'd be used by someone so close to me."

The warmth from his hand had her softening her words, and Paisley could feel herself melting little by little. The wall of defense she had so firmly in place was slowly slipping away.

"I never intended to hurt you," he stated. "Yes, I saw you as a way to get to Sterling, but the man is a complete bastard. I volleyed between wanting him to be your dad so you'd have closure and wanting him to not be your dad because I didn't want you to have anything to do with the jerk."

He slid his free hand to the other side of her waist and pulled her closer until their torsos aligned. Even rumpled and haggard, Lucas Ford was the sexiest man she'd ever seen.

Sexy wasn't going to win her heart over, though. But that pain in his eyes, a look that she'd never experienced, and the pleading were doing a damn good job of getting her attention.

So much for being made of steel and making him grovel.

"I went and saw my real dad," she told him. "He's...sick."

"I know, but I'm glad you're getting time together now."

Paisley closed her eyes and pulled in a deep breath. "I can't be with you if I can't trust you."

"I know that, too," he countered. "But I plan on spending every day for the rest of our lives making you see that I love you more than anything."

Paisley's heart clenched. "What?"

"I love you," he repeated.

He dipped his head and captured her mouth, gently at first, then he coaxed her lips apart. Paisley arched against him and opened, her body instantly responding to his touch. All warning flags dropped. She didn't want to focus on the negative. She only wanted to focus on the fact Lucas had come because she was hurting—and to tell her he loved her.

His hands slid around the silky robe and beneath the hem to her bare backside.

"Damn, Tart," he muttered against her mouth. "You're naked."

"I was going to get in the shower," she whispered. "I didn't plan on company."

He rested his forehead against hers. "Let me in," he commanded. "Your neighbors are getting a show."

Totally caught up in the moment, in the man, she'd forgotten they were standing in her doorway for the whole street and anyone walking by to see.

Paisley gripped his shirtfront and tugged him into her foyer. He dove right back in, devouring her mouth as his hands went to the tie on her robe. The material parted and his hands were on her. Finally.

"I've missed you," he growled against her mouth. "I need you so much."

Yeah, she had some pretty desperate needs of her own.

Lucas gripped her ass and lifted her against him. Paisley wrapped her legs around his waist, then held on as he turned and sat her on the accent table at the base of the staircase. He immediately stepped between her spread legs and yanked the robe down to her elbows, trapping her arms against her sides.

"Tell me you want this," he demanded. "I want to hear you say it."

Paisley nodded, trying to form a sentence when her body was aching. "I want you, Lucas. Now."

He released the robe and palmed her breasts as she laced her fingers through his hair. She scooted forward on the cool tabletop and locked her ankles behind his back.

His hands fell away and she felt him fidgeting between her legs followed by the sound of his zipper. He circled her waist with his large, strong hands and stared into her eyes as he joined their bodies.

Paisley cried out as her body arched, her

head dropping back. Lucas slid a hand around to the small of her back for support as he pumped his hips and murmured something she couldn't make out.

His lips grazed over her breasts, along her neck, and she tipped her head back so he could take her lips. Her fingertips dug into his shoulders and she gripped the fabric of his shirt, wishing he would've removed it so she could fully touch him.

"Paisley," he murmured.

Hearing her name on his lips, seeing that tightening of his jaw as if he was barely holding on to his control, had her body spiraling out of control. She tightened all around him and let the moment consume her.

Seconds later, Lucas tightened his hold on her waist and dropped his head to the crook in her neck. Paisley ran her hands over his shoulders, to his neck, and into his hair, cradling him as his pleasure took hold.

After several moments, when their bodies settled, only their breathing filled the space. Paisley wondered if she'd made a mistake letting him in so soon. She hadn't made him grovel too much and she was pretty sure she hadn't even made him use the four and a half minutes.

She'd always been weak where Lucas was concerned, but now she had to figure out how to handle this. Yes, she wanted him, but she had to trust him.

"Don't start having doubts."

Lucas felt her pulling away. Oh, not physically. She was still wrapped all around him. Emotionally and mentally, she was already rewinding and trying to come up with something to say and some way to protect herself.

"This can work," he added. "I know I made a mistake that could cost me everything, but I'm here to tell you that I won't put anything above you ever again."

He eased back and smoothed the hair away from her face. The thought of letting her go hurt him to a level he couldn't describe and didn't want to comprehend. He didn't even want to go there in his own mind because he was going to do anything in his power to show her he was in love with her.

"I'll buy you a wedding dress." The words were out before he thought twice, but then he realized she deserved so much more. "Any dress. I don't care if it's hand-beaded, or whatever that expensive one was, or if you want to recycle that lace thing. I want to give you the wedding of your dreams."

Paisley laughed. "I'm never wearing that jumpsuit again and you put so much money in my business account, I don't need you to buy me anything."

He'd put that money in her account because he didn't want her to worry about finances even for a second. He'd secretly contacted the jilted bride and he knew the insane wedding gown had ultimately been paid for in full after he'd reminded the customer she was in breach of contract.

If Paisley ultimately decided to leave him, Lucas would be absolutely devastated, but he still wanted to provide a solid security for her and pave a smooth path in her life.

Paisley sighed. "I can't keep that money, you know. And great sex won't fix our problems."

Lucas took a half step back and adjusted his pants, but left them unbuttoned. He eased the silky robe back up her arms and covered her breasts.

"I swear I did not come here for sex." He wanted her to know she was so much more to him. "You're everything to me. I'm here because I wanted to fix your hurt, if that's even possible. I know I did damage, but tell me what I can do to make it right. There's nothing I wouldn't do for you."

Paisley bit on her bottom lip as her eyes darted away. She eased off the table, causing him to take another step back to give her space. Lucas watched as she righted her robe, but the silence was absolutely maddening.

He had nobody to be angry with but himself, but he couldn't go back in time and have a redo. At this point, all he could hope to accomplish was to get through to Paisley that he really did have good intentions, he just executed everything the wrong way.

"Family is everything to me," he told her. "I wanted vengeance for my father. I had been waiting for the right opportunity to get back at Sterling, so when he went to jail, I was thinking that would have to suffice, though I had nothing to do with that. But then you walked in and my first thought was, what if it's true? What if you do belong to him? I won't lie, I wanted you in my bed. I was more than eager to have you all to myself while I investigated."

Paisley crossed her arms over her chest, but didn't make a move to step away or shut him out. Lucas took that as a good sign and kept going.

"But then you moved in," he said. "Having you in my space, even with the yellow throw pillows and those pictures you call art, I realized I wanted all of that there because that's who you are. I wasn't still hung up on some young love. I was falling for the woman you are now."

Her eyes misted and she glanced down, but Lucas took his hand and lifted her attention back to him.

"Don't hide from me," he said. "When you feel something, anything, I want you to share it with me. And I'll do the same. There's nothing I want to do alone anymore. Tell me you'll think about us, think about not leaving for good. I'm willing to start over, I'm willing—"

"Shut up."

Lucas froze. "Excuse me?"

Paisley blinked, causing a tear to slide down her cheek. "I told myself to let you grovel for a long time, but I can't handle it anymore."

She'd told herself...

What the hell?

Lucas framed her face and swiped at the tear with the pad of his thumb. "Did I grovel long enough?"

Paisley shrugged. "I'm not sure yet. But I needed a break."

He kissed her lips, quickly, softly. "I'll spend the rest of my life groveling if you give me the chance. Let's make this a real marriage and start a family."

She smiled. For the first time since he'd set foot in the door, she offered a true, genuine smile.

"I wouldn't have let you in, let alone had sex with you, if I didn't want to give you another chance."

Paisley's delicate arms came up around his neck and Lucas wasted no time in pulling her closer. "I don't deserve you," he murmured.

"You don't," she agreed with a laugh. "But we're legally bound, so you're stuck with me."

"Fine by me." He nipped at her lips once

again. "I believe you said something about a shower earlier. Do you have room for one more?"

"In my shower and in my heart."

Lucas swept her up into his arms and carried her up to the second floor. This next chapter of his life was going to be the best yet. He may not have gotten revenge like he'd wanted, but he got something so much more fulfilling. He had the only woman he'd ever loved and soon, they'd have their own family.

Nothing compared to that.

# Epilogue

Angela swept into the café and weaved her way through the tables. Lavinia sat in the back and lifted a hand to wave Angela over.

"So sorry I'm late," Angela said as she pulled her chair out. "Traffic was a nightmare."

The waiter came by and Angela ordered a water as she set her bag beneath the table and took a seat. She inhaled deeply and stared across the table at her friend.

"It's so good to see you," Angela stated. "We don't do lunch often enough."

"We don't," Lavinia agreed. "So much has been going on with your dad and then there's that body that has still not been identified. Everything is so crazy lately."

Angela cringed. "I can't even wrap my mind around that poor person who died. I mean, they had a family somewhere that is no doubt wondering where their loved one is. Nobody deserves to just…"

"I know," Lavinia muttered her agreement.

The waiter came back with water and took their order before leaving them alone again.

"On a brighter note," Lavinia said. "You're absolutely beaming. Something must be going right for you."

Angela pulled the cloth napkin from the table and smoothed it over her lap. "You could say that. With all the upheaval in my life, Ryder and I have decided to get away from it all and take a trip. Just the two of us. We really need the time alone to just reset."

Lavinia gasped. "Oh, my. You are one strong woman. I admire that. I don't know what I'd do if the man I was dating was rumored to have fathered my brother."

Angela stilled, and her heart clenched as the breath caught in her throat. "What?"

"You haven't heard?" Lavinia asked, her eyes wide.

She took a sip of her water and leaned forward as she spoke lower. "Ryder is rumored to have had an affair with your mother and he's actually Roarke's father, not Sterling."

Angela gripped her napkin in her lap, suddenly feeling quite nauseated. The affairs were nothing new, but she hadn't heard the most damning rumor. No doubt Lavinia, the town gossip, was all too eager to share the tidbits she knew.

This couldn't be true. There was no way Ryder was Roarke's father. That couldn't be. There had to be some mistake.

Angela couldn't even gather all her thoughts that were swirling through her